HANGDOG III
The Absolution

Book Three of the Hangdog Trilogy
By: Tylie Vaughan Eaves

D1569505

Vertū Publishing, 2019
A Component of Vertū Marketing, LLC

VERTŪ PUBLISHING

A Component of Vertū Marketing LLC

www.vertu-marketing.com

Ordering Information:
Quantity sales. Special discounts are available on quantity purchases by corporations, associations, and others. For details, contact the publisher at the address above.
Orders by U.S. trade bookstores and wholesalers.
Please contact: Tel: (866) 779-0795.

Printed in the United States of America

ISBN 978-0-578-59088-2

DEDICATION

This book is dedicated to my sweet uncle, Sammy "Sambo" Fanning. I can't wait to see your face again. I can't wait to hug your neck. My longing for Heaven is even stronger now, simply because you're already there.

Joshua 1:9

July 19, 1972 – March 13, 2019

Death is Just a Doorway

Death is just a doorway to the place called Paradise.
Oh, if you could only see it, you wouldn't believe your eyes!
I'm already busy, I have so many things to do. And I'll be here with Jesus, loving, laughing, and waiting for you.
I've seen so many loved ones. I've hugged my brother again. It wasn't what I expected, oh, but what a way to win!
I won't ask you not to cry, at least not for today — but I will ask you to remember happy times, and that you laugh along the way.
I will ask that you stay strong. Press on like I would do. Don't give up, don't give in. You have a job to do.
Be the hands and feet of Jesus. Love each other every day. Fight the good fight, be the light, and battle on, come what may.
It won't be long until I see you again, oh, and when I do, I'll hug you tight, in the Father's light, and I'll be so proud of you.
For now I have to go, just know I love you so. Remember that death is just a doorway. I'm on the other side. I'm happy and I'm healthy — Forever.
SEMPER FI

Hangdog III – The Absolution

PART ONE

CHAPTER ONE

Andy could feel his heart beating in his throat as he drove like mad through the night, his headlights cutting through the darkness as he made his way toward the nearest emergency room. His stomach churned as he looked into his rearview mirror every two seconds in a feeble attempt to assure himself that his closest friend and brother in arms would be alright. Beau was motionless, face down, in the bed of Andy's truck, covered in vomit and sweat.

Andy drove fiercely, going as fast as he dared. He could feel the perspiration beading on his forehead as he struggled to beat back the feelings of panic and fear welling inside him. As he glanced into the rearview mirror for what seemed like the thousandth time, he caught a glimpse of his own reflection and paused for a split second, taken aback. The fear in his own eyes was obvious, his brow was furrowed and the muscles of his tightly clenched jaw were bulging beneath his smooth skin — it was an expression he had never before seen on his own face.

When his mind registered the look of fear in his own eyes, he became instantly frustrated with himself. He inhaled deeply. "What am I doing?" He looked into his rearview mirror once again. "Get yourself together Andy! What is wrong with you? God is the same today as He was yesterday and the day before and you know it! You know it!" He took another deep breath, reminding himself again of the power and goodness he'd already seen in Beau's life time and time again, and he resolved that fear would not win over his faith — not this day. "No!" he shouted at the top of his lungs as he began to pray aloud with a fiery passion he couldn't contain. The prayer flowed through him, as though coming from somewhere else. He called out to God on Beau's behalf, loudly, boldly, and expectantly. Soon, his sense of peace had returned, but he prayed on, quietly proclaiming God's blessing on his own life, as well as on Beau's. Over and over again, he quoted scripture to himself, strengthening his own faith with God's word. "He doesn't give us the spirit of fear. He is not the author of confusion." Andy surprised himself when he felt tears fill his eyes. He was not a crier, but something about the gravity of the moment was more than even his steadfast emotions could bear.

He reached up with his right hand and rubbed his eyes with his thumb and forefinger. As he lowered his hand back to the wheel, preparing for the next turn toward the hospital, he glanced again into his rearview mirror and jumped, totally startled by the site of Beau's moving form in the reflection.

Beau was pushing himself upright in the bed of the truck, pressing his torso up with his arms as he struggled against the movement of the vehicle. The street lights danced off the sweat on his face and hair. Andy's shock was perforated only by his sense of urgency. He didn't register, or even consider, what an abrupt stop would do to Beau as he pulled to the shoulder of the road almost violently, making the turn and hitting his brakes in one swift movement. Beau was forcefully rocked to one side, losing his balance just before he fell forward into a pool of his own vomit. Andy threw the truck into park and jumped out, urgently yelling, "Beau! Hangdog, are you okay? McKnight, can you hear me?"

Beau was slowly pushing himself up again, "Yeah, yeah, I can hear you. Stop yelling." He sounded confused, but also frustrated. He pulled his legs under him and was sitting on his backside, his knees bent in front of him. He moved his left hand to his head. "Where are we? What's happening?" Beau's head throbbed. "And *what* is that smell?" he asked as he gagged.

Andy inhaled deeply, silently thanking God. "You've pulled through for me again, Lord. Why do I ever doubt you?" He looked at Beau. "That smell would be you." He stopped for a single beat before continuing, "You've been sliding around in your own vomit for the last fifteen minutes."

"What?" Beau was wiping his face with his hands, disoriented.

"You overdosed Beau — or something. You were having seizures and puking and you wouldn't wake up. We were on our way to the hospital." Andy stated calmly. The peace in his spirit had returned, and his heart was soaring with gratitude. He told Beau the unvarnished truth about the night's events without adding extra drama or flair, in typical Big Mack fashion.

Beau dropped his head between his knees, as far as his injured, and now throbbing, shoulder would allow. "No. No hospitals!" he stated emphatically. "I can't go to a hospital. I'm okay. I'll be okay now."

Andy knew Beau's world hung in the balance, and taking him to a hospital now could ruin him as a Marine and could even land him in jail. He didn't push the issue, but he'd already decided that, because eternity for Beau also hung in the balance, he'd do whatever had to be done to ensure his life was spared. Jail time held no candle to an eternity in hell, separated from God. "There's something else," Andy murmured as he took a ragged, drawn out breath. He really didn't want to tell Beau about the baby, but he knew he needed to, knew he had to. "Julia went into labor. We couldn't find you. Eli and I had already searched for you the entire afternoon when we got word you'd gone to that party, but by the time we found you, it was too late. Eli went on to the hospital and I stayed to help you."

"What? No!" Beau kept his head down. "Did I miss it?" He cursed under his breath. "Did I?" His whole body ached. He couldn't believe he'd missed the birth of his son. He couldn't believe he'd screwed up again.

Andy hesitated, "Well, she was already starting to push when Eli left. He was going to cover for you as best he could." He held his breath for a second, "I'm sorry man." Andy didn't know what to say, but he also didn't want Beau's emotions to get the better of him and make the night even worse. "But maybe we still have time," he tried to sound optimistic. "Let's get you cleaned up. Maybe we can still make it."

Beau didn't speak, but he nodded slightly. Andy wasn't sure, but he thought Beau was holding back tears. "Okay, so, the cleaning up part. I don't know what to do." He thought for a moment. "I've got a T-shirt and some shorts in the truck, you can wear those. Hopefully, they'll fit."

Beau let out a pained grunt, "Zippy's is up the road. I can wash up, and you can rinse off the truck."

"Okay." Andy looked at Beau, sheepishly. "So, are you okay to, um, you know, ride back here?" He made a face. Beau was covered in vomit. The smell was intense in open air and Andy couldn't stomach the idea of being in closed quarters with it.

Beau just nodded, his head still hanging, too sad and dejected to say anything.

~

Inside the gas station bathroom, Beau stared at himself in a dirty mirror. The florescent light flickered above him as he let the cool water run over his hands. Though he'd washed his face, he still felt like he looked dirty. He gently patted the raw, strawberry like scrape on his cheek. The rough bed liner in Andy's truck had nearly rubbed a hole in his skin. He took a ragged breath, eye to eye with a person he didn't recognize. "What is wrong with you?" he wondered as he stared at his face. His mind raced through a Rolodex of stored thoughts, sticking again and again on one single point — all he'd wanted for so long was for Eli to be awake, happy and healthy. And now, he had exactly that, everything he'd hoped for, and more

— but somehow, he still felt hollow. Somehow, he still felt like a failure. He stared at his reflection until he didn't recognize his own face. And then, without warning, his new son was at the center of his thoughts — he needed to get there. He didn't understand his sudden sense of urgency, but his *need* to get to Julia and the baby was almost overwhelming. He hurriedly pulled a paper towel from the dispenser and used it to dry his hands. He dampened a second towel under the faucet and wiped the back of his neck before tossing both into the trash.

Andy's T-shirt fit him snugly, but it was clean. The shorts were snug too, and even a little shorter than Beau preferred, but still better than the vomit-coated alternative. He walked out into the bright lights of the convenience store, his clothes wound tightly into a ball. He made a bee-line for the counter and requested a plastic bag before putting a pack of gum onto the counter. He looked over his left shoulder to the gas station parking lot and saw Andy's wet truck sparkling under the lights. It hadn't taken long to wash away the remains of the night, and if not for his bag of dirty clothes and his throbbing headache, there was no remaining physical evidence of what had just transpired.

As Beau exited the shop, Andy rolled down his driver's side window and held out a bottle of water in Beau's direction. Beau reached out and took it. "If you don't mind, leave that bag in the back," he said with a slight smile in his voice. He patted the side of his truck with his hand and continued, "Now let's go meet your son!" Beau made sure the bag was knotted tightly and placed it gently into the bed of the truck, up near the cab. He moved quickly around to the passenger side and pulled up on the door handle with his left hand. Once inside, he opened his pack of gum and popped a piece into his mouth. He gave Andy a silent signal to get moving and the pair set off toward the hospital.

The ride was largely silent. Neither of them knew exactly what to say. Andy spoke silent prayers of thanks every few minutes. The night could have gone so very differently, it could have been so much worse, but God's mercy had seen them through a nightmare — and Andy knew it. After a few minutes of dead silence, Beau spoke. "I'm sorry," he murmured. "About tonight I mean. All of this." His head was hanging again and Andy nodded, willing the Holy Spirit to give him the right words.

Finally, he responded, "I don't need your apology. I have your back, no matter what. You know that. What I want to know is if you're sorry enough to finally get your *own* back?"

There was a long pause before Beau finally spoke, "What?"

"You know exactly 'what.' I'm looking out for you, Eli is looking out for you, your parents are looking out for you, Julia is looking out for you — the only person not looking out for you, is you! I want to know if you're finally sorry enough to join the effort?" There was no anger in Andy's voice. His tone was as calm and even as ever, but his words clanged in Beau's ears like a gong.

Beau said nothing. Instead, he stared out the passenger side window, watching the night pass by. He wanted to defend himself, but he didn't know how. The harder he thought about a reason for his choices, the more ridiculous he felt. It seemed like he punctuated every good thing in his life with a stupid choice, and he didn't know why. He thought back to high school, and the risks he'd taken in the name of fun, but when he looked back, even the fun he had didn't seem all that *fun*. For years, when he hadn't been actively pursuing some expected accomplishment, like football, he'd spent his hours chasing the next good time — the next high.

As he stared into the darkness, he had to admit to himself that, when push came to shove, that chase had cost him his football scholarship, and it had cost Eli two years of his life and probably his relationship with Ivy. In fact, Beau's chase had almost taken Eli's life completely. He thought about the grief his parents had endured, the stress they'd been under and the financial burdens they'd endured all because he'd made selfish choices. Now, even Andy and Julia were paying the price for his choices — and soon, if he didn't get his act together, his son would suffer the same fate. But how? How did he fix this?

Beau laid his head back against the seat. He didn't make mistakes on purpose. He didn't make bad choices intentionally. It was almost like he lacked the power to stop himself. How could he continue to hurt the people he loved time and time again, even after he'd been blessed to see miracles over and over again? Eli was back, whole and healthy. He himself was alive. He was in love and was about to become a father. He'd found success and he'd done things he never thought possible — why wasn't that enough? He felt somewhat emasculated at the idea that everyone in his life was looking out for him, except himself.

As Andy made his final turn into the hospital parking lot, right outside the entrance to the labor and delivery unit, Beau spoke, "Look, I don't know why I do what I do, okay. It's not like I'm a screw-up on purpose. I just am one."

"Says the guy who has excelled at everything we've ever done together. You're *not* a screw-up. Screw-ups aren't good at everything they do." Andy put the truck in park and turned the key off before turning to look at Beau.

"Well, then, apparently, I excel at screwing up, too." Beau looked at him, straight-faced.

Andy couldn't help but smirk, "Listen, I just think it's time you loved yourself as much as the rest of us do. That's all. Or better yet, just recognize how much God loves you and start from there.

CHAPTER TWO

Julia couldn't slow her tears as she looked down at the tiny miracle resting in her arms, swaddled in a white blanket, wriggling ever so slightly against her chest. There was lots of hustle and bustle in the room around her, but in that moment, only her son existed. She was in awe of his small head and sweet fingers. She gently pulled the infant cap from Gabe's tiny head and pressed her lips to his skin, breathing in his scent and feeling the softness of his peach-fuzz hair against her cheek. "Look at you," she whispered. "You're just perfect, aren't you? Just so perfect." She closed her eyes and said a silent prayer of thanks to her newfound Savior, fully acknowledging her blessings and, for the first time ever, sensing a purpose for her life beyond herself.

Eli stood across the room, silently watching his mother gush and take photos, while Julia's mother wiped tears from her eyes and gently stroked Julia's hair. Julia looked beautiful. He looked at tiny baby Gabe in Julia's arms and thought to himself, "Beau should be here." Inside, Eli was a ball of conflicting emotions. He was overjoyed and angry at the same time. He felt peace and concern at the same time. Where were they? Was Beau okay? He checked his phone again. Nothing. He sent Andy yet another text. He then texted his brother's phone as well. What could it hurt? <WHERE ARE YOU?>

As the doctor and nurses finished up with Julia, Eli heard a light tapping on the door off to his left. He glanced around the room, but no one else had seemed to notice. Everyone was either busy with Julia or cooing at baby Gabe. Eli walked the few steps toward the door, opened it slightly, and peeked out. On the other side, he saw his father's beaming face. One of the nurses must have told him about Gabe's momentous arrival, because he was grinning from ear-to-ear. Eli opened the door to allow his dad to come through. As Joe walked past him, Eli instinctively looked out into the hallway. Except for a few nurses, the hall was clear. Under his breath, he whispered, "Where are you guys?" Eli turned back into the room and watched as his dad knelt by Julia's bed. He pulled his phone from his pocket and checked his messages one more time — just in case. As he slid his phone back into his pocket, his mom urged him to join his father by the bed. She wanted more pictures. Eli stepped around Joe and knelt behind him, smiling. Three photo's later, it was Val's turn.

"My turn," she sang. "Eli, come use my phone and take one with me in it!" Valerie was radiant with joy. She was in love already and everyone who looked at her could tell. She was going to spoil that baby like no grandmother had ever spoiled a baby in the history of grandmothers.

As Eli started to stand, Julia reached up with her left hand and touched his face gently with her fingers. "Thank you for being here, Eli," she said softly, sincerely, her eyes sparkling with both tears of joy and gratitude as she gave him a soft smile. When her eyes met his, Eli felt an unexpected, shocked jolt. He was mesmerized and taken aback at the same time. Without warning, he felt something *different, something he shouldn't feel,* when he looked at her.

Guilt welled up inside him, but he didn't know why. His mind recoiled. This shouldn't be his moment, wasn't his moment — he was living Beau's moment. But somehow, at the same time, he was happy about it. He didn't want to be anywhere else. It thrilled him and terrified him at the same time. He smiled slightly and nodded toward Julia, unsure of how to respond to her, of how to process the strange, internal battle raging in his heart. As he moved toward his mother, his thoughts shifted from Julia, the baby and his brother, to Ivy.

The touch of Julia's hand had somehow shocked his wounded heart. Perhaps it was because Ivy had been the only person to brush his cheek like that, ever — until now. He closed his eyes and tried to shake off the strangeness he felt. He did his best to laugh and talk and smile, but his mind bounced from thought to thought uncontrollably.

Eli took a few more pictures with his mom's phone, and then pulled out his own. Still no messages. He took some more pictures, and as Julia handed the baby over to her mother for some more photos and "bonding time with grandma," as she'd called it, he found himself focused on her. She was beautiful, glowing. For a moment, Eli was mesmerized by the soft curves of her face and the genuine joy shining in her eyes. He'd seen pretty girls all his life, but up until now, Ivy had been the only one to hold him spellbound. Eli believed wholeheartedly in the difference between *pretty* and *beautiful*. And Julia was beautiful.

"Stop it!" he shouted to himself. He willed himself to look away. "What are you doing? What are you thinking?" The thoughts in his head were screaming at him. He closed his eyes, embarrassed that he was even thinking of Julia in a different way, in that way! "What's wrong with you? She literally just had your *brother's* baby." He mentally urged himself to snap out of it. Guilt swept over him again. Did he really have feelings for Julia? No, surely not. He looked at her again. She was smiling up at Joe, who had just kissed the top of her head. Except for one nurse, the room was devoid of hospital staff. Eli hadn't even noticed them leave. He took a deep breath and let it out slowly. He'd always expected to share a moment like this with Ivy, but now, for the first time since she'd ended things, he wasn't even missing her. Was it Julia he wanted? Or was it simply the moment he envied? "Let it go," he told himself, as he spoke a silent prayer, "What's happening here, God?"

As he closed his eyes in desperation, the door to Julia's room shot open. A short, rather robust nurse with a clipboard in one hand and a portable coffee cup in the other came bursting into the room. Her voice was boisterous and somewhat low pitched. She somehow sounded sarcastic even though she wasn't being sarcastic. "Well, look what the cat dragged in." Beau came into the room sheepishly behind her, followed closely by Andy. "Mmm-hmm," she said. Better late to the party than never, right honey?" she asked Beau dismissively, as she turned on her heels toward the door. She clearly had no intention of waiting around for an answer.

Eli fell back into the recliner in the corner of the room and looked up toward the ceiling. He breathed a deep sigh of relief and gave thanks to God that Beau seemed to be okay. He exchanged a knowing look with Andy, who walked toward him and placed a hand on his shoulder.

Beau moved slowly and tentatively to Julia's bedside. He expected her to question him about where he'd been, but she didn't. He bent over her and kissed her gently before kneeling down beside her. He lifted his left arm to grab her hand, doing his best to balance without putting weight on his injured shoulder. Julia's mom walked over and gently laid the baby in her arms. Beau felt his breath leave his body, "Oh, wow. Oh, he's so tiny."

"He's perfect," Julia returned, looking up at Beau with a smile. Beau rose to his feet, bending over Julia's bed to get a better look at his son. As he did, Julia took note of the raw skin on his cheek. "Oh, my goodness! What happened to your cheek?" she asked with genuine concern.

"Oh, that. It's nothing. Just an accident. Never mind about me — how are *you*?"

Julia laughed, "I'm exhausted! But I'm doing pretty good, considering."

"She did great, hon," Val chimed in to give Julia some praise. "You would have been so proud of her."

"I'm so, so sorry I didn't get here in time." Beau hung his head, hoping nobody would ask him where he'd been or why he didn't answer his phone. He hadn't taken the time to think up a plausible excuse on his way to the hospital. "I…"

Julia cut him off, "Never mind that, you're here now. It's time for you to meet your son. Do you want to hold him?"

Beau was taken aback. He'd expected Julia to be angry, or at least upset. Instead, she seemed so peaceful. He assumed it was the exhaustion, the medications, or maybe the sheer fact that she had just become a mother, but then, she spoke again.

"Isn't he a miracle?"

When Beau heard her words, he remembered the news she'd given him earlier. For a split second, he wondered if her newfound peace was a result of her newfound faith, but he chose to wipe this idea from his mind for now, he wasn't ready to think about it. Valerie moved closer to help Julia lift Gabe into his father's arms. Beau peered down at the baby's smooth skin and tiny features. He could feel Gabe breathing as he slept. He looked perfectly content and comfortable. Beau felt an overwhelming sense of responsibility pour over him, just as if he'd stepped under a stream of falling water. He became instantly consumed with the thought of protecting his baby and providing for Julia. Love for them both swelled in his heart — you could see it in his eyes. It now felt different. It now was somehow more real to him. He'd never felt love like this and he knew there would be no going back. He blinked back tears as he kissed Gabe's little head. "I'm your daddy, young man," he whispered. "I've got your back from this day on, every minute, and don't you forget it."

His entire family watched in silence, soaking in the moment. It was almost as if they watched him soften before their eyes. He transformed into a father. Val leaned into Joe as she lifted her hands to wipe her teary eyes. Julia smiled and sniffed back tears of her own. Julia's mom let out an audible sound of approval. Joe spoke up then, deciding to lighten the mood, "I'm pretty sure I heard myself speak when you said, 'young man.' Poor kid." He laughed at himself and everyone chuckled.

Beau turned to face Eli and Andy in the corner of the room. Eli looked at him and smiled, but Beau could see something brewing behind his eyes. He knew they'd have words soon. He knew there was no denying the night's events. He'd have to face it. He shifted his gaze to Andy, who had a serene look on his face. Once he made eye contact with Andy, he nodded. Only Andy knew what it meant, and he smiled. Beau pressed his lips together and nodded again. It took that moment. It took his son, sleeping in his arms, to push him toward the answer Andy wanted — he was ready to change!

~

Eli couldn't help it. He found himself watching Julia as she watched Beau. Jealousy welled inside him, and he seemed powerless to stop the feeling. "What is happening to me?" His mind recoiled from his thoughts. Where was this feeling coming from? He lifted his palms to his face and pressed the heels of his hands into his eyes. He forced himself to admit that his newfound affections for Julia weren't as sudden as he'd like to think. Since his release from the hospital, he'd spent time with her almost every day. He'd gotten to know her. She had such a kind spirit, and it didn't hurt that she was beautiful — even at her largest, with swollen ankles, she could easily turn heads. And now, she shared his faith. Is *that* what pushed him over the edge?

He forced himself to look up again. Beau was placing baby Gabe back in his mother's arms and posing for yet another picture. Julia looked up at Beau and he leaned in to kiss her. Eli wanted to look away, but he made himself watch. "What's happening to me?" He willed himself to think about Ivy, but his stomach churned as he found himself unable to focus on anything but Beau and Julia. "I'm losing it," he told himself silently. Julia was, is, and always would be Beau's girl. Even if they hadn't reconnected, if it had ended for good in middle school, she'd still *always* be Beau's girl. Eli's stomach churned.

He needed to get out of this room. "I think I'm going to go downstairs and get something to drink," he announced. "Anybody else want something?"

Andy, who had been smiling since the second he'd walked through the door, spoke up, "That sounds good. I'll go with you." The pair took drink orders from Valerie and Joe and Julia's mom, and Andy gave Beau a knowing look before asking, "Water?" Something in the tone in his voice made it sound like a loaded question, and Eli heard it immediately.

Beau nodded and answered, "Thanks." Andy knew the word held a double meaning and he shot his friend a knowing look in response.

~

As soon as they cleared the double doors of the maternity ward, Eli turned to Andy. "Well? What happened?" he asked impatiently, desperate to think about anything except his sudden obsession with Julia.

"Well," Andy sighed, "right after you left, he had a seizure…"

Eli cut him off, "What?!"

"Yeah, I was just about to call out to God when he started shaking all over. I was more scared than I've ever been in my life." Andy wiped his mouth with this hand. "I was taking him to the hospital when I remembered that fear isn't God's doing, so I pulled myself together to pray, and well, God stepped in from there."

"Wow!" Eli stared at his feet, shaking his head as they walked. "I'm really glad it was you who stayed with him."

"As opposed to you, you mean?" Andy asked.

"I just don't think I have faith like that."

"You do too have faith like that. Every believer has faith like that. It's just a mustard seed. The difference is most people seem to balance out their faith with equal amounts of unbelief. I mean, we're surrounded by it all the time. It's up to us how we process it. People are programmed to think things have to be a certain way, when they don't." Andy slapped Eli's back with this palm.

"Programmed, huh?" Eli asked. He'd have to think about this some more.

After a few minutes of discussing the arrival of the newest McKnight and how miraculously the entire day had turned out to be, the pair walked along in silence. Eli wanted to focus on his gratitude, but he was so angry with Beau, and now with himself, that he couldn't seem to focus. Andy, who was silently celebrating not only the birth, but yet another miracle on Beau's behalf, began to sense that something was wrong with Eli. "What's in your head right now, Uncle Eli?"

"Nothing," Eli murmured.

"Right." Andy's voice dripped with sarcasm as he cocked an eyebrow in Eli's direction. They turned the corner into the corridor outside the cafeteria and Eli felt himself grow nauseous. How was he going to avoid this subject?

"Really, it's nothing." Eli shoved his hands into his pockets again.

Andy shrugged. He knew something was bothering Eli and wanted to help. "I can't make you tell me, so you just let me know when you're ready." Andy paused for a moment before adding, "Are you ready now? How about now?"

"Oh c'mon! I'm just mad at Beau, okay? I mean, how could he do that to Julia — to any of us?" There was no way Eli was going to tell Andy the full truth. He had no intentions of telling anyone. He was having enough trouble admitting the truth to himself — not only was he mad at Beau for choosing booze and pills over his family, but he was also struggling with guilt because of some kind of sudden, unannounced, and unrequited love for Julia.

"I get it," Andy responded, even though Eli knew he didn't get it all.

"I mean, I was there when his son was born," Eli said vehemently. "Me! It should *not* have been me. It should have been him. How could he? And he lied to us! He told us he would stop with the pills, but he didn't, and frankly, I don't think he ever intended to. So, now what? I'm just supposed to pretend I didn't see what I saw tonight? We're supposed to ignore that whole terrifying scene? Pretend it never happened? And what about Julia? She's supposed to go home and raise a baby with an addict and not even know it? She's too good for that. Too good for *him*! And don't even get me started on the baby. I mean, imagine if Beau was your dad. Give me a break." He blurted out his words like a firehose of emotion, spouting his anger and exasperation.

"I don't think we are supposed to ignore it. But I don't think we should out and out condemn him for it either." Andy took a breath, "I don't think he makes bad choices on purpose, and deep down, you don't think that either. He's lost Eli, and lost people make lost choices. If you were lost in the desert, you'd do anything for water — Beau is lost and trying to fill a void. That's it. It's our job to help him find the way. We can't let our disappointment in his lostness derail our mission to help him find his way."

Eli sighed deeply. He wanted to argue with Andy's perspective, but he couldn't. Andy was right. "Andy, bro, you're twenty something, not seventy something. Why do you go all wise sage on me all the time?" he laughed.

Andy laughed too, but asked, "So you agree with me then?"

"I guess," Eli said grudgingly. "I mean, yeah, yes, I do. But I don't have to like it." Eli blew another breath out through his lips, this time forcefully. His stomach was in knots. Thinking of Beau, lost, trying to fill a void he didn't even know he had with whatever he could get his hands on seemed to magnify Eli's thoughts about Julia, as well as his guilt.

"I think he's ready to change. I think he's becoming more open to faith," Andy added.

"What makes you say that?" Eli asked.

"His face when he saw his son." Andy looked at Eli. He told the truth, but not the whole story. He didn't intend to share his earlier conversation with Beau. Not because it was a secret, but because something about it felt personal.

"I hope you're right," Eli shook his head. "Julia and the baby deserve the best. You know, before he came home from the hospital, I spent every day with Julia, every single day. She's an amazing person, and now she's a mother, and she's also a believer. Can Beau take care of her, of them? Can he be what they need?" Eli tried his best to sound at least a little indifferent and shrugged his shoulders.

Andy watched him from the corner of his eye as they moved toward the drink machines. Eli sensed Andy's questioning gaze and felt his face flush. "I held the baby, you know. I cut the umbilical cord. He's just incredible, and he's my nephew, my blood. I just want to make sure Beau does right by him." Eli was hoping that, maybe, mentioning baby Gabe would somehow blind Andy to his unexpected and inexplicable new feelings for Julia and the strange and sudden jealousy he now felt toward his own brother. It seemed to work. Eli sighed with relief when Andy looked away and began filling cups with ice.

"You saw his face," Andy said. "He'll do right by that baby and by Julia too." He glanced at Eli again. "If becoming a dad doesn't motivate him… well, I mean, he has a reason now — and God's still knocking. Let's just pray he opens that door." Andy slapped Eli's shoulder with his right hand, hoping that the intensity of the night's events had simply taken a toll on him. Eli seemed off, but Andy ignored his gut instinct and chalked it up to exhaustion and worry.

Eli nodded. He tried to shake the mass of tangled thoughts from his mind. Maybe all he needed was a good night's sleep. Maybe he was just delusional from exhaustion. Maybe he'd wake up tomorrow and forget all about Julia. As he tried to focus on the simple task of getting drinks, he found himself distracted by the idea that, for what felt like a long time, all he'd wanted was to forget Ivy. He'd prayed to forget her. But this wasn't what he had in mind. This wasn't the way he wanted to do it. In this instant, he'd give anything to pine for Ivy again, anything, *if* it meant he could let go of his unwanted feelings for Julia. Eli looked at Andy, "Let's get these back upstairs. I think I'm ready to head home. I'm beat."

Andy smiled, "Sounds good to me. It's been a long day."

CHAPTER THREE

Andy hauled a large basket of his own clothes down the stairs, heading for the laundry room. The house had been a bustle since the newest McKnight had joined the ranks, and Andy had let his laundry pile up. Valerie had offered to do the wash for him, but she and Joe had done so much for him already, it didn't seem right. He knew his leave would soon come to an end, and with it, his time with the McKnights. Though he wasn't emotional by nature, the pending goodbye was already painful. So much had happened since he'd arrived at the McKnight home. Life somehow felt completely different, and there was even a brand new person in his life. Baby Gabe had stolen hearts from the minute he'd made his debut, and Andy's was no exception. As he reached the bottom step and made the turn to pass through the great room, the doorbell rang. Andy paused, waiting to see if anyone else in the house would come running. Then he remembered that Julia was napping with baby Gabe, and he decided he'd better answer before the bell rang again.

Andy lowered his basket to the floor and took the few steps back toward the stately front door. As he pulled the door open, he took note of a wide-eyed, dark-skinned young man staring up at the eaves of the house with his mouth hanging open. "Um, hi," Andy said.

"Oh, uh, sorry. Hi. My name is Antonne. I'm looking for a Joe McKnight. Do I have the right house?"

"Antonne!" Andy opened the door a little wider. He'd been hearing about Antonne for weeks now. He felt like he already knew the guy, but given Beau's description, this Antonne seemed far less obnoxious than the one he'd expected. "You're in the right place. I'm Andy. Mr. Joe and Mrs. Valerie have been expecting you, but they didn't know exactly when."

"Truth is, I didn't know either." Antonne dropped his duffle bag on the porch and extended a hand toward Andy. Andy took it and moved aside to clear the way for Antonne's entry. As Antonne made his way into the house, the astonishment on his face became obvious. "I ain't never seen a place like this in all my life," he said, looking at Andy with amazement on his face.

Andy smiled, "It's pretty nice, right?"

"Nice?" Antonne chuckled. "My dorm room was nice. This is, like, wow! If I'd known 'ol Hangdoggy was a prince, I'd have tried harder to get here." Antonne laughed heartily at his own joke. Andy couldn't help himself, there was something about Antonne that struck him as funny. He laughed too.

"Well, I guess I'll round them up. I don't even live here."

Antonne glanced at the laundry basket by the door. "What, are you their butler or somethin'? Dang, I *am* moving up in the world."

Andy laughed again, "No, no. I'm in Beau's unit. He's like a brother to me. I'm just here on leave."

"Oh," Antonne drew the word out long. "Andy. Andy. Andy." He repeated Andy's name several times, out loud, in what appeared to be an attempt to remember if he'd heard something about him during his time in the hospital with Beau. "Yeah, man. You're Jesus Andy!" Antonne nodded emphatically at his own recollection and added, "Good to meet ya."

If Andy was surprised at being called Jesus Andy, he didn't let on, as he picked up his laundry basket and said, "Follow me." He moved through the great room and kitchen, with Antonne trailing slowly behind him. Antonne took in his surroundings like he'd just entered the Taj Mahal. When they reached the kitchen, he got a glimpse of the back deck and the pathway down to the pool and he stopped in his tracks.

"Bro, is that a pool?" he asked excitedly.

"Yep," Andy laughed.

Antonne's face lit up. "I tell you what, son, I'mma like it here." He danced briefly to an apparent victory tune playing only in his own head and added a drawn out "Ooooh."

Andy smiled, having already decided he liked Antonne. Andy continued through the kitchen and down the short, wide hallway to the laundry room and placed his basket on the washing machine. With Antonne following closely behind, he made his way to the next door. He opened the door, which led down to the basement, where Joe, Val and Eli had been preparing for Antonne's arrival. They weren't exactly sure when he'd arrive, but Val had wasted no time making the basement into the perfect guest unit. She'd been replacing the linens, stocking the cupboards in the basement kitchen, decorating, and moving furniture. Well, the boys had been moving furniture, Val had been telling them where to move it.

"Guys," Andy called down the stairs. "We have a guest." The words came out seamlessly, just as if Andy were a McKnight himself. He heard himself say the words and smiled, because he knew that everyone else felt the same way too. Andy was part of the family, and they all loved him.

"What?" Eli called back. "Who?"

Both Andy and Antonne heard Joe say, "Grab that hammer," before yelling, "We'll be right up."

Antonne was right on Andy's heels and he was already at the bottom of the stairs when Andy added, "We're coming to you." They reached the bottom step and turned into the room. Antonne was smiling from ear-to-ear as he turned the corner. He was genuinely excited to see them. Something about them made him feel safe.

"Antonne!" Valerie trotted across the room and reached out to give him a famous Valerie McKnight hug. At first, she'd had her doubts about Antonne moving in, but as Joe had continued to cultivate a relationship with him, she found herself not only warming to the idea, but becoming sincerely happy about it. Antonne placed his bag on the floor and returned her hug. To him, it didn't feel strange or off-putting. His personality lent itself to matters of the heart, and it seemed as though the McKnights were the family he'd always wanted, but never had.

Valerie took it upon herself to extend a hand toward Eli, "This is Beau's brother, Eli." Antonne moved closer to Eli and held out his hand. Eli took it in a handshake, "Nice to meet you, Antonne. I've heard lots about you. I feel like I know you already!"

"Wow!" Antonne replied before adding, "I heard a lot about you, too, but when Hangdog said 'brother,' I didn't know he meant *twin* brother!" He smiled broadly as he shook Eli's hand.

Eli laughed, "Yeah, we're twins, but I'm still better looking."

Antonne chuckled and shook his head, "Wow. It's crazy. And, on top of it, I'm standing here shaking hands with a real life miracle!"

Joe stepped closer to the two young men and laid a hand on Eli's shoulder. "Walking miracle is right," he said. He looked intently at Antonne. It had been months since they last saw each other, but Joe had been in communication with Antonne almost every week, "Well, welcome home, son." Joe reached out to shake Antonne's hand, and then he gestured toward the surroundings they'd literally just finished perfecting.

"Wait, really?" Antonne saw the small, but updated kitchen, the wrap around couch and the big screen TV on the wall. He took in the walk-out French doors that looked as if they emerged onto a shaded veranda, with latticework on one side, a table and chairs, and even a porch swing. Valerie, who had a God-given talent for hospitality, had placed potted plants strategically around the patio and Antonne couldn't keep himself from walking toward the doors to look out. He could see the pathway to the pool and hot tub, "No way. No way. Are you serious?" The excitement in his voice was obvious.

"Come this way and I'll show you the bedroom and the bathroom. And right through there is what we call the 'game room,' but it's really just a pool table and the place we store board games." Valerie literally sang the words as she gave her house tour. She loved her home. She took great care in making it as warm and inviting as possible, and she truly enjoyed welcoming guests. Her care and love was evident in every detail. Every inch was impeccably decorated and spotlessly clean. "And right there is the 'home gym,'" Valerie laughed immediately after she spoke the words, because the home gym consisted of nothing more than her treadmill, a yoga mat, a small set of hand weights, one exercise ball and a television mounted on the wall."

"I'm blown away. This is just too much to believe!" Antonne turned toward her as she gestured into what was now his bedroom."

Val smiled, "Go ahead and put your bag down, hon. You can unpack later." She paused, "Oh my. I bet you need to use the bathroom, huh? It's kind of a haul to get here from the airport!" The bathroom was directly across the hall from the gym area. "This light can be tricky. The one closest to the door is for the wall sconces over the sink, the middle is the overhead light and the pot light in the shower, and the far one is the heat lamp. It is just outside the shower, and if you accidently hit it while you're just in here getting dressed or something, you'll cook." She laughed again. "That little door there is the throne room. There's extra tissue paper and towels under the sink. Oh, and this little feature is one of my favorites." She walked across the room to a shiny rack against the wall. "It's a towel warmer. If you hit this little button here, it will warm your towel while you shower. I just love that!" Antonne's mouth hung open. He looked around the room at the gleaming granite counters and intricate tile work. The tiled shower had double heads, a teak bench and what looked like body jets. He'd never seen anything like it in real life. There was a vanity cabinet against one wall, with rolled towels and candles on top. On the far wall hung a full length mirror and beneath it rested a tufted bench that looked like something he'd seen in a magazine once.

Val looked like she might speak again, so Joe quickly interrupted, "Let the boy pee in peace, Val!"

"Oh, right!" She chuckled. "I'm sorry!"

"I'm speechless. I really am. I mean, this is just too much."

"Well, that's a first." Beau stuck his head into the room. After going to the kitchen for a snack, he'd found the basement door open and had come down to investigate. When he heard his mother giving her enthusiastic tour, he knew immediately Antonne had arrived.

"Hangdog!" Antonne sounded genuinely happy to see him. He dropped his bag and took a few steps toward Beau, and as Beau came around the corner, Antonne threw both arms around him, as if they had a deeper bond than Beau thought they had. Beau patted his back.

"Hey, hey. That's enough of that," he spoke jokingly, but inside he wondered why Antonne seemed so glad to see him. Beau had never even been nice to him, not really.

Andy, who was standing nearby with a huge grin on his face, was already beginning to like Antonne. The look on Beau's face when Antonne hugged him made the moment even sweeter. Antonne's presence would be good for Beau.

"We'll let you get settled in," Joe interjected.

"Yes. Let's get out of Antonne's hair for a few minutes, let him get unpacked. I'll start prepping dinner in a little while, if anyone feels like chopping some onion," Val added.

Eli gave Andy a little shove to his shoulder and laughed, "Andy's really good with onion."

"But weren't you just telling me the other day how much you loved chopping vegetables? Here's your big chance!" Andy gave Eli a playful shove in return.

"Last one to the kitchen is the onion cutter," Eli added.

"You're on," Andy answered. The two took off immediately, heading for the stairs. They pushed and shoved and ran and laughed and laughed some more.

Valerie couldn't help but see them as little boys, just as she always had. It didn't matter how old they became, to her, they'd always be little boys. "Be careful on the stairs!" she called behind them.

Beau shrugged and started up the stairs after them, slowly. "I'm pretty sure onion cutting would aggravate my bad shoulder." He winked at his mom as he grabbed his right shoulder and over-dramatized a pained look. Val giggled and shook her head before heading toward the stairs behind him. She paused at the bottom, waiting for Joe.

Joe turned to Antonne. He started to speak, but as he turned, he saw Antonne standing in the middle of the room with tears in his eyes. Joe didn't get the chance to open his mouth before Antonne tearfully spoke up, "Thank you, Mr. Joe. Thank you so much, for all of this. I… I've never…"

Valerie heard Antonne and started crying immediately. She didn't think it was possible for her to love Joe more than she already did, but in that moment, her love for him took on new life. It had been his call to invite Antonne into their home. He'd seen the need. He'd been willing to sacrifice his privacy, his football-watching space, the place he and his boys called their mancave, all so a young man with little could become a young man with a lot. Her practical, logical husband had listened to the still small voice in his spirit and had opened his heart to a kid he barely knew, and now she was witness to the byproduct of his obedience. Her heart was bursting with both pride and gratitude. She regretted her doubts. She regretted pushing back when Joe first talked to her about it. She walked across the room and laced her arm through Joe's. Joe felt her presence at his side. He struggled to find words and he refused to cry. "Think nothing of it, son. We're very happy to have you here. Welcome home." Joe walked toward Antonne and raised his arms to hug him. Antonne welcomed the embrace and cried on his shoulder. Valerie moved with him and wrapped her arms around them both as the tears streamed down her face. When Joe finally pulled away, Antonne wiped his eyes with his hands and sniffed. Joe cleared his throat, clearly holding back tears of his own, "Come up whenever you like."

"I'll cut onion and anything else that needs cutting," Antonne said, smiling, his wet eyes shining in the light. Val touched his face with the tenderness only a mother can display. Joe smiled. He had experienced moments of doubt in his decision to invite Antonne to live with them, especially when he considered Val's reservations, but those doubts had now totally evaporated. As he watched Val watching Antonne, he was certain — Antonne was exactly where he was supposed to be.

CHAPTER FOUR

Eli hadn't realized he was staring at Julia until she turned her head and caught him. He quickly looked away and wanted to kick himself for not only staring, but for getting caught. Since she'd arrived home with Gabe, Eli's sudden and unexplainable feelings for her had only seemed to intensify. His stomach churned at the thought. He felt both jealousy and guilt at the same time.

At one point, he had come very near to telling her the truth. They had both been in the laundry room, working side by side. She was folding a load of her clothes while Eli loaded his own. Val's decision to put a small TV in the laundry room had been a game changer for the household laundry cycle and, as they worked, Julia and Eli had watched a daytime talk show. They'd laughed and chatted and Eli had come so close to blurting out his feelings for her that he'd been avoiding her ever since. Now, sitting in the kitchen as she and Val worked on dinner, he knew he had to tell her the truth.

He was terrified, but it was all he could think about. He felt certain he could keep it hidden from everyone else. After all, he'd done a good job of it so far, but every time Julia was around, he felt compelled to tell her. He watched her moving around the kitchen. She was beautiful, somehow even more beautiful than she had been before Gabe was born. Maybe it was her newfound passion for her faith. Maybe it was the fact that she practically glowed with love for her baby. Maybe it was none of these things. Maybe he had simply lost his mind. He sat in silence, trying to think of a way to tell Julia how he felt — without ruining his relationship with his family, especially his brother. He thought, maybe, if he could just tell her, and her alone, that no one else needed to know and maybe, just maybe, he'd feel better. Eli chuckled softly to himself as he contemplated the irony of his situation. He thought he'd never get over Ivy. He thought he'd be broken-hearted forever. He spent day after day hoping to forget her. But then, Julia — and wham! Now that he could only think of Julia, he'd give anything to pine for Ivy again.

"Eli, did you hear me?" Eli vaguely registered his mother's voice.

"Snap out of it boy!" Joe chimed in, laughing.

"Oh, sorry, I was… never mind. What's up?" Eli tried to act as casually as he could.

"Will you set the table, please?" Val requested.

"Oh, sure." Eli stood up from his seat and moved toward the familiar cabinet where the dinner plates had been stored for as long as he could remember. After he finished counting out the plates, he moved quickly, placing one at each spot around the table. When he was finished, he moved to a separate cabinet, which happened to be located just above Julia's head by the refrigerator. Julia stepped back slightly and let Eli reach over her. Eli could feel his heart pounding in his chest as he stood closely beside her. He felt certain it was beating loud enough for her to hear it too. He took two glasses out of the cabinet and placed them on the counter. Before he could reach in for two more, Julia joined him to help. The back of her hand brushed his as they both reached into the cabinet. He breathed in sharply and held his breath.

"I'll help with these," Julia said as she moved a glass toward the ice dispenser on the fridge.

Eli could hardly speak, but he forced out the word "Thanks," before pulling the remaining few glasses from the cabinet. "That's it," he thought to himself, "I can't live like this. I have to tell her."

~

Dinner was typical, just another meal. But since Antonne had arrived, every family meal was full of conversation and laughter. Of course, Andy's impending departure had become a normal part of the daily conversation. He would be leaving in a few days' time and his parents had made plans to drive up the coast to meet him back in North Carolina. They wanted to see Camp Lejeune and hang out with their son before he had to get back to work. Andy was looking forward to some time with his parents. He needed to talk about life. He'd been a Marine long enough that it was time to consider his future. He loved the McKnights, but they already had so much *life* happening with their own kids, it didn't seem right to bring up his own issues. Plus, no one could replace his own mom and dad.

Still, every time he thought about leaving, he felt a little sad. He felt torn. Though he was ready to get back to work, he wasn't ready to leave — not just because he loved being with the McKnights, but because of Beau in particular. Beau had been struggling to fight his addiction by himself, in relative secret. He didn't want to talk about it. Any time Eli questioned him, Beau would become defensive and angry. Andy knew he hadn't stopped using, not completely, and leaving him now felt almost like a betrayal.

"I made brownies!" Valerie stood up from the table and went to the stove, where she'd left a pan of fresh brownies to cool.

"Yes!" Antonne exclaimed, like a little boy.

"I second that!" Joe added.

Valerie walked the pan to the table and turned back toward the coffee station. Joe loved a cup of decaf with his evening dessert, so much so that Valerie made it without even asking anymore. Baby Gabe had fallen asleep in Julia's arms and Beau reached for him, "I'll put him in his swing. That way you can double fist some brownies." He winked at Julia, who laughed. Eli felt heat rise in his face. He willed himself to be happy for his brother, but his willpower was no match for his mounting jealousy.

"Well, my sweet boys," Valerie said as she poured Joe his cup of coffee. "I simply can't believe you'll be twenty-one on Thursday! Twenty-one! Can you Joe, can you even believe it?"

"I'm pretty sure I'm still twenty-one, so I don't even think it's possible," Joe chuckled.

"I'd say I feel more like twenty-five or thirty, but still not old enough to have sons who are officially *in* their twenties," Val laughingly added.

"I've been meaning to ask you about that Ms. Valerie," Julia spoke up.

"I was hoping that, since Andy is leaving on Friday, hmm… " Julia cleared her throat. She felt right at home with the McKnights, and she and Val had grown very close, especially since she'd grown so passionate about her faith, but she still hated to ask for favors. "Maybe after we finish with the birthday dinner on Thursday, you might babysit for us, so we can take Andy out that night too." She smiled toward Andy, "Sort of a going away party and birthday combo!"

"I think that's a great idea!" Val exclaimed immediately. And it was true that she thought it was a great idea. It would be fun for all of them. They hadn't done much of anything since Gabe was born, and without Ivy, Eli had become a homebody. But, if she was being truthful, her eagerness had less to do with her boys and more to do with the baby. "I guarantee half the family will want to cuddle that sweet little pea all night, but I will happily run them off and keep him all to myself!"

"All to yourself, huh?" Joe retorted sarcastically. "I see how it's going to be. Well, believe me beautiful, I ain't going down without a fight."

Val laughed, "He's all mine, Joe. This is one fight you're gonna lose!"

"I don't think a domestic dispute was part of the plan you two," Eli added dryly.

"Yeah," Beau added. "Maybe we should just take him with us," he winked at Julia. "These two can't be trusted."

"You shut your mouth Beau McKnight. That baby adores me!" Val laughed and gave Beau a light poke to the chest.

"He loves me more though," Joe mumbled under his breath, and then started laughing at his own joke.

Val shook her head playfully. "Either way, it's settled. We'll have the family over for a birthday meal around five thirty, then we'll keep our little Gaby while you guys go out and have some fun and show our Andy just how much we'll miss him around here." She smiled in Andy's direction.

"Thanks, Ms. Valerie," Andy smiled back. "It's going to be tough to leave."

"Any idea what's going to happen next for you, son?" Joe asked, looking intently at Andy.

"No, sir. Except I'm pretty sure there's another deployment coming my way. I'll have just barely over a year left on my enlistment, so I'm not sure what I'll do from there.

Not sure if I'll reenlist or what. I haven't heard from God just yet, so we'll just wait and see.

The mention of passing time weighed heavily on Beau. He ached over how much of his deployment he'd missed and how many months he'd spent recovering and in rehab. And now, to be waiting even longer felt like a slap in the face. So much time had already passed that he questioned whether or not he could still call himself a Marine. That thought took him to a dark place — a place he was trying hard to forget.

Beau's shift in mood was almost palpable, at least to Andy, so he decided to change the subject. "So, what kind of magnificent outing do you have in store for me Miss Julia?"

Julia giggled. "Well, I haven't gotten that far yet," she laughingly said. "I thought I was doing pretty good to get this far! I swear, my brain still feels like mush. How long does it take pregnancy brain to go away?" The way she asked her question with just a tad bit of seriousness and a whole lot of sarcasm made Joe laugh hilariously.

"Well," he said. "It's been right at twenty-one years now, and Val still struggles." He spoke the words as if he were deadly serious and then looked down at the table trying not to laugh. Then he made the mistake of looking up at Val. The expression on her face was so hilarious, he began to laugh out loud. Just listening to Joe's guffawing caused Antonne to burst out laughing. Andy was quick to join in, with Eli following closely behind him, and then Julia. All that laughing pulled Beau's attention away from himself and his problems and back to the present, and he found himself laughing too.

Val sighed and then let out a laugh of her own. "As much as I hate to admit it, it's kind of true. Becoming a mom *does* seem to make you a little stupider — for-ev-er! I blame the exhaustion." She leaned over toward Beau and grabbed his hand. "Totally worth it, though. They're so, so, totally worth it." She smiled at Eli and then gave Beau's hand another quick squeeze.

CHAPTER FIVE

Eli paced back and forth inside his room, trying to build the courage to walk down the hall and tell Julia the full truth about how he felt. His stomach churned inside him. Every time he thought he had mustered the guts to speak up, he thought about Beau, and how much he loved him. Imagining how this would make Beau feel if he ever found out made Eli's heart ache with guilt. If Beau knew the truth, things between them would never be the same. But, at the same time, if he didn't tell Julia how he felt, he knew it would drive him crazy. He felt like an intense pressure was building up inside his spirit, and the only way to relieve the pressure would be to open the valve and tell her the truth. He didn't know why he *had* to tell her, but he couldn't eat, he couldn't sleep, and he couldn't stop *needing* her to know. He knew nothing would, or could, become of it. He knew there was no future with Julia. She belonged to his brother, and Eli felt both jealous and, somehow, comforted by that fact at the same time. He wiped his hands on his pants and tried to talk himself out of it. His effort was in vain, because every time his rational mind told him to keep his mouth shut, his heart overpowered his brain and telling her became his only option, and the only thing he could think about. But, with every passing second, one thing was for certain — Beau must never, ever find out.

Finally, after catching a glimpse of his own reflection in the mirror, Eli willed himself to make a move. He stared at himself in the mirror and told his reflection, "This is stupid. Stop being such a baby. Get it over with." He smoothed back his hair, wiped his face with his hands, and turned to open his bedroom door. He knew that Beau had gone to his physical therapy appointment and that baby Gabe was napping. Now would be the perfect time for an uninterrupted conversation with Julia. He stepped out into the hallway and turned his body toward Julia's room with militant purpose. Valerie was out back working in the garden, Andy and Antonne had gone out, and his father wouldn't be home from work for another couple hours. He likely wouldn't get another opportunity like this one, and he was bound and determined to take it, regardless of how terrified he felt. He hadn't realized he'd been holding his breath until he found himself standing outside Julia's door. He slowly released the air from his lungs and took a deep breath, willing himself to knock. All that was left to do was knock. He closed his eyes, squeezing them shut in silent determination, and raised his fist, knocking lightly on the door three times.

"Come in," Julia called out sweetly. Eli could hear the sounds of her television playing in the background. He cleared his throat and turned the knob, stepping in over the threshold. Julia was sitting cross-legged on her bed surrounded by small stacks of neatly folded clothes. "Hi! I'm going through my drawers. A lot of this stuff doesn't fit right now, but I hate to get rid of it. I'm trying to organize it so what I actually wear is easier to get to. Hopefully, I won't be fat forever!" She laughed to herself before asking, "What's up?"

"You are not fat." Eli's response was immediate. He decided to take a chance and added, "You're beautiful."

"Aw, thank you! You are the sweetest!" Julia smiled at him and Eli felt his heart began to pound inside his chest.

"So, can I talk to you for a minute?" Eli could hear the hesitation in his own voice.

"Of course." Julia tried to hide her confusion. Somehow, she felt a little like she'd been called to the principal's office — or like she was about to receive bad news. When Eli stepped toward the door and closed it behind him, she became increasingly concerned. "Is everything okay? What's wrong?"

"Everything's fine. I... I just need to talk to you in private." Eli pointed to an empty spot on Julia's bed, as if asking for permission to sit down.

"Yes, sit," Julia nodded as she spoke. "Just tell me what's going on! The suspense is already killing me!" She laughed again.

"First, I think it's important for you to know that what I'm about to tell you comes with no strings, expectations or, well, anything really. I honestly don't expect anything from you. And I think it's very important that you know I'm only telling you because I can't physically keep it inside anymore. Believe me, I've tried." Eli shifted uneasily on the bed.

Julia grabbed the remote from her nightstand and muted the TV. "Oh, my goodness. Eli, what's going on? I'm officially freaked out right now." She looked at Eli, and then quickly, instinctively, took a peek inside the bassinet. Gabe was sleeping peacefully, and she turned back to Eli with a look of urgency on her face.

Eli closed his eyes for a moment and took a deep breath. Somehow, he was both comfortable and uncomfortable at the same time. "I'm just going to come out with it... I don't know any other way to do it." He cleared his throat and continued, "Julia, I... I can't stop thinking about you. Ever since, ever since the hospital — ever since I saw you holding baby Gabe for the first time, I literally can't get you out of my head. And not in the way you think. I mean, I mean it's not platonic. It's not the kind of 'in my head' one would expect with a sister. Do you get what I'm saying?"

"What?" Julia's voice was breathy, and she was clearly confused. Her forehead crinkled and Eli could see that his message wasn't getting through.

"Oh, okay. What I'm trying to say is, I think I'm in love with you. Or at least I'm falling in love with you. At least, that's what it feels like. I don't know how else to explain it. My stomach is in knots whenever you're around, my palms are sweaty, my heart beats fast. I can't stop staring at you, I can't stop thinking about you, and I can't deny the fact that I am absolutely sick with jealousy every time I see you with Beau." Eli spit the words out abruptly, like they were hot coals in his mouth, but, somehow, he also said them tenderly. When he finished speaking, there was a long pause. Julia neither moved nor spoke. Total shock blanketed her face. Finally, Eli spoke up again, "I don't expect anything from you. I know my feelings aren't going anywhere. I know a relationship between us is out of the question. And I don't think I want to know if you could ever feel the same way about me because, either way, the answer would torture me." He paused again, took a deep breath and looked down toward his feet. "I don't want Beau to ever,

ever find out about this. He can't know. I love him, and he would hate me if he knew how I felt about you. But, I had to tell you the truth because not telling you simply wasn't an option. I haven't been able to sleep because it felt like I might die every minute I didn't tell you. I can't explain it. I don't understand it myself. It would have been so much easier to just love you in secret. But, here I am." He looked her in the eyes, allowing a thick, awkward pause to settle in between them before he added, "Say something."

Julia jumped up from her seat on the bed and took a few steps across the room, placing a hand over her mouth. She started to pace. "I… I don't know what to say. I mean, are you kidding me, Eli?" Julia whispered, as if afraid someone might hear her. She took a deep breath. "Why would you… what are you thinking?" She paced some more, still letting the feeling of shock and disbelief settle within her. She looked over at Eli, whose eyes were still cast downward toward his feet. He looked like a scolded little boy and instantly her heart ached for him. Eli was exactly the kind of man she *should* want to be with. He was literally everything a girl could want. She'd never let herself see him that way, but now, she had no other choice. Finally, she thought of something to say, "You know what I think?" She said the words as if they were somehow going to solve a problem, like she'd had an epiphany. "I think maybe you're still heartbroken over Ivy. I don't think you can trust your feelings right now. I think your emotions are playing tricks on you."

"Trust me, that's not it." Eli looked up at her again. "I have wanted nothing more than to think about Ivy these last few weeks. I've literally *tried* to think about her — but I can't. Because when I close my eyes, it's *your* face I see," he smiled hesitantly. "I've practically run away from you every time I've seen you, because it was all I could do not to yell it out."

Julia paused again. She thought back to all the nights they'd spent together while she was pregnant, and all the times Eli had listened to her talk about her fears. She recalled how many times he'd brought her ice cream without being asked and how he'd always let her control the remote and pick the movie. Once, when she was complaining about how enormously swollen her ankles had become, he'd set up Valerie's old footbath for her — without being asked — and then he sat with her while she soaked her feet! Who does that? Surely, by anyone's standards, Eli McKnight was a total keeper. Unfortunately, she wasn't *anyone*. She did her best to gather her composure. "Eli," she moved close to him and took his hand in hers. "You know I am in love with your brother. You know it. Yes, in a different world, you might be the perfect guy for me. But, in this world, Beau is my soulmate. He always has been. He has his flaws, God knows, but I do love him. He's the father of my child, and someday, I hope to be his wife. I hope you can understand that. I..."

Eli cut her off, "Stop, you don't have to... I know. I know all of this. I knew all that before I walked in here. Like I said, I didn't tell you because I wanted to change your mind. I'm not trying to take you from Beau or win you over. I don't want to. I really don't. He loves you and you love him. I know that. I just... I just needed *you* to know how I feel. I don't know why. I can't explain it. But maybe by telling you, I will find some relief and finally be able to get some sleep." He laughed at his own words, partly to make himself feel better and partly to take some pressure off Julia. "This is not something I want you to worry about. It's just that I need you to know how special you are. You are loved, and will be loved, no matter what." He squeezed her hand, his heart flopping inside his chest like a fish out of water at the touch. "I don't want to make things hard for you. That's not my intention. I just had to tell you. I'm sorry."

Julia still couldn't believe her ears. The moment seemed like a dream or like a movie that, somehow, she'd been thrust into, but she cared for Eli — she hated to see him in torment, even if it did make her feel good in a selfish kind of way. "There's nothing to be sorry about. I'm glad you told me. I love you, too — just, you know, in a different way." She smiled at him and leaned over to hug him. She placed both arms around him, and he wrapped his arms around her in return. She could feel his heart beating in his chest and she smelled the scent of his cologne. She kissed his cheek.

Eli finally spoke again, "And we agree? Beau never hears about this — ever."

"Agreed." Julia hated keeping secrets, especially from Beau. But, for the sake of both Beau and Eli, and for her, too, for that matter, this secret would most definitely go with her to her grave.

As Eli stood to leave, Julia thought about Beau. She knew she'd made the right choice in reaffirming her love for him, but she couldn't help but imagine for just a moment what life might be like if she somehow ended up with Eli instead. She stood and walked Eli to the door of her room. She was still lost in her daydream when he turned back around to face her, "Jules?" The sound of her name on his lips startled her back into the present. "Thank you." Eli smiled at her and then turned to walk back down the hallway to his room.

After he left, Julia closed the door to her room and then wiped her face with her hands. "What just happened?" she asked herself as she sat back down on the bed. She took a deep breath and couldn't help feeling flattered and, well, flabbergasted. Regardless of what she'd told him, Eli did make her feel good about herself. It was nice to feel desirable and to feel wanted, especially during a time when she felt anything but beautiful. But feeling flattered also came with a pang of guilt. Was she *allowed* to feel flattered by his affection? She prayed to herself out loud, "I'm pretty sure *this* is *not* in my Bible, Lord." She knew she'd have to be careful around Eli going forward, and that she needed to be cautious of his heart — but that didn't stop her from being glad she knew the truth. She moved a stack of shirts to the edge of her bed and did her best to shake the surreal moment from her mind so she could get back to work. As she did, she prayed again, "God, please help me to always do what's right. Show me your plan, so I can follow your lead and not my own."

Back inside his room, Eli fell face first onto his bed. He couldn't decide if he felt better or not, at least not right now. He felt mortified, but also relieved. As he lay there thinking about Julia and how caring and kind she'd been to him when she could have easily rejected him or laughed him out of the house, he began to feel sleepy. He hadn't really slept well since the night Gabe was born, and now that Julia knew the truth, he was finally going to get some rest — maybe the truth really would set him free.

CHAPTER SIX

Andy had been driving around Longview for hours, doing his best to show Antonne around, despite the fact that he was essentially a stranger to the town himself. Most of their time had been spent learning the lay of the land together. Andy liked Antonne. He'd liked him from minute one, and today's excursion had only solidified his feelings. Something about Antonne was infectious, and the fact that he hadn't stopped talking since the moment he'd climbed into Andy's truck only made Andy like him more. And, of course, it made Beau's complaints about him funnier than ever. At one point, Andy found himself laughing under his breath right in the middle of an epic Antonne tale. There was nothing funny about the story, but in Andy's mind he saw Beau sharing a hospital room with Antonne and living in confined quarters with the most upbeat, talkative person Andy had ever met. When he thought about the contrast between Beau's personality and Antonne's, he had to laugh.

After a few hours of driving around, the pair decided it was time to stop for a late lunch. Andy rolled into the parking lot and found an end spot. He swung his truck out wide and pulled into the spot, being careful to pull his truck as close to the curb as possible, leaving more room on the passenger side. As they climbed out of the truck, Andy heard God speaking to his spirit. It was very clear to him that God wanted Antonne to be there for Beau. The idea of leaving, knowing that Beau was struggling with the secret demon of substance abuse, had kept Andy up at night more than once. The socially acceptable thing to do would be to keep his mouth shut, after all, it wasn't exactly his place. But Andy knew in his heart that God wanted him to share the struggle with Antonne. He trusted Antonne to step in and be there for Beau come what may.

Andy and Antonne followed the hostess to a corner booth on the bar side of the small Mexican restaurant they'd chosen as their lunch destination. After getting settled in, taking bathroom breaks and placing drink orders, they practically inhaled a basket of chips and a bowl of salsa before their waiter came to take their order. Antonne seemed overly excited at the prospect of a double-stuffed cheese and chicken quesadilla and

French fries, a fact that made Andy laugh yet again. Andy ordered two beef burritos and a side of rice. As the waiter placed another basket of chips on the table, he cleared his throat — bound and determined to do what God was telling him to do. "Antonne, I really need to talk to you about something. In the little bit of time I've known you, I've learned that you're a man of faith, at least from what I've picked up." Some of the things Antonne had said made it clear to Andy that he was a believer, but he somehow knew that because of Antonne's past, he struggled with the concept of faith and a God he didn't understand, a God who didn't always intervene to prevent bad things from happening. Andy knew that it was a common misunderstanding of how God works and who God is, but he'd never successfully changed anyone's mind. It was something a man had to learn for himself. Andy prayed a quick, silent prayer that, in time, Antonne would develop a hunger for truth and take it upon himself to open up to the true nature of God. As far as Andy was concerned, there was no better place to do that than in the McKnight household. "You admit you don't have it all figured out, and that's okay, because I still know you'll believe me when I say that God wants me to share this stuff with you. The problem is, I'm pretty blunt. I don't do well dancing around the point, so I don't try. I don't want to freak you out, but it's important that I get this out."

"Dang, Andy. I'm kind of scared now," Antonne chuckled, but stopped when the look on Andy's face made it obvious that he wasn't being sarcastic. "Okay, what's up?"

"Like I said, I'm pretty blunt. I'm just going to come out with it, so brace yourself." Andy took a deep breath and then began, "Beau has a drug problem. He won't come out and say he's addicted, but he is. He's hooked on the prescription pain pills they started giving him after... Well, you already know that part of the story." He cleared his throat. Antonne sat silently, holding a chip a few inches from his mouth frozen in midair. Andy continued, "On the night Gabe was born, he found out his medical board was going to be on hold for more evaluation. He left Eli and me and went to some house party where he got hammered drunk and took a number of pills only God could know. When Julia went into labor, Eli and I ran all over town searching for him, when we found him, he was passed out on a dirty couch in the back bedroom of a rundown house on the other side of town." Andy told Antonne the whole, sordid story. He gave all the details he could about the people involved, where they hung out, everything Antonne might need to know should Beau ever go missing again.

Antonne's eyes were huge. He had a deep admiration for Beau, and he wasn't even sure why. They'd only met in the hospital, but Antonne saw strength in Beau and looked up to him in some strange way. He found it almost impossible to believe that *the* Beau McKnight had this kind of problem. Beau was always so rigid and hard. Antonne gave him a hard time about his chronic bad mood, but deep down, he also kind of admired those qualities in Beau. They kept him reliable. Andy's words sort of felt like a story, or a movie — but at the same time, they felt too familiar. "I gotta be honest," Antonne said. "Bro, that's a lot to take in. It doesn't seem right. It doesn't fit who he is — or at least who I thought he was."

"You're right, it doesn't fit with the *image* of who Beau "Hangdog" McKnight, gruff, stoic, golden-boy of the Marine Corps, should be. But then again, when you think about it, it does fit. See, Beau doesn't have Jesus. He struggles with faith. He's been wrestling with God ever since I've known him. He's trying to kill the pain, not just in his body, but in his soul. And lost people make lost choices. Eli told me that Beau has always been a partier, well, since high school anyway, but said he was never an idiot. Eli said Beau liked to drink, but that he never did drugs. Obviously, Eli is not doing good with this situation. He's angry, really angry. And who could blame him? And, after getting to know his family, I've learned that Beau is a completely different person than he was before Eli's coma. I've only ever known him to be the way he is now, and I knew when I met him that he was the way he was for a reason. That means you've only ever known him one way too. But apparently, that one way is not who he started out to be. Supposedly, Beau McKnight used to be full of life and, at the same time, the life of every party. He used to be the jokester, funny, always happy, having a good time and making other people laugh. Then, after Eli, well…" Andy took a sip of his drink and shrugged.

Antonne had his mouth covered with his hand, listening intently, deeply invested in what Andy was telling him as their waiter set the food down in front of them. Andy bowed his head to pray. Antonne had already put a bite on his fork, but when he saw Andy, he followed suit. He looked back up at Andy as he put the fork full of food in his mouth, then raised his eyebrows and nodded in Andy's direction, willing him to continue. He knew there was more. He gestured toward Andy with his fork and, with his mouth full, said, "You were sayin'?"

"Well, on that night, while we were trying to get him to the hospital so he could be there when his son was born, he began throwing up all over the place and he wouldn't open his eyes. But I knew he'd never forgive us if we took him to the ER." Andy proceeded to tell Antonne about the choices they made that night, the words they spoke and Eli's torn heart over the whole thing. No detail was left unspoken. "And then, as I was starting to call on God to intervene, he had a seizure. Scariest thing I've ever seen, and I was *with* him in the desert!

For a little while, I let the fear take over. I left him in the back of the truck and rushed toward the nearest hospital. I figured that alive and jobless was still better than dead. But then as I drove, I realized that I had let the fear win. Fear ain't from God, Antonne. Remember that. So, I cast it out. I took control of my emotions and I prayed like I've never prayed before. And God came through for me again — for Beau, just like he's done so many times before." Andy began to smile as he finished his story, "It nearly scared me into the ditch when I saw his face rise up in my rearview mirror!"

Antonne was riveted, he chewed silently, hanging on every word. He laughed at the mental picture of Beau's face in the rearview. He swallowed, "Man, you're the most calm dude I've ever seen in my whole life. I ain't known you long, but I ain't blind either. I can't imagine you gettin' worked up about anything."

Andy shook his head, "I did that night."

"Then what happened?"

"Nothin' really," Andy answered. I got him cleaned up, ran my truck through the wash, and took him to the hospital. We did talk though, you know, about all of it." Andy took a big bite of his burrito, trying to mind his manners despite his full mouth. "I asked him if he was ready to step up, to change. He didn't come out and answer, but I saw his face when he looked at that baby. He's ready to stop. It's just that…"

"It's just what?" Antonne asked, still trying to get his head around the firestorm of information he was taking in.

"It's just that I don't think he can stop," Andy sighed.

"You know, I grew up in a bad way. I never knew my dad. My mom, well, she did whatever she had to do for money, but all the money went right up her nose. I was just a little kid, but I knew I didn't want that for myself. I knew that life didn't have to be my life, so as soon as I was old enough, I got out. I've never had much, I've never been much, and way back then there was nothing I could do to stop my mom from doing what she did." Andy saw Antonne's eyes fill with tears. He wiped them quickly with the back of his hand and sniffed hard, as if his tears were an unexpected foe. "I don't even know where she is now. I got nobody there, and then the McKnights… Mr. Joe and Ms. Val, they're proof God is real, you know what I'm sayin'?" Andy nodded, a slight smile on his face. Antonne stiffened up, "I'll be da…" he stopped himself before the word came out. Something about being with Andy made him want to be a better man, "I won't stand by and watch it happen to Beau. He's too good for it. And I can't watch it. I can't. And that baby — it just can't happen."

"I feel sure that God brought you here when he did because Beau's gonna need you, Antonne. I feel it in my spirit. You're here for a reason — a reason bigger than yourself."

Antonne's expression grew pained, "What? What can I do?"

"Just be there. You'll know what to do when you need to do it. Trust God to tell you." Andy took another sip of his drink.

"I can't hear God like you do, man. He don't just chat me up on the regular. We ain't tight like that." Antonne laughed at his own words, but he was speaking the truth.

"You can be though. That's up to you," Andy said matter-of-factly.

"Right," Antonne said sarcastically.

"I'm serious. It's your choice. And, if I'm right about Beau and where this all might lead, you'll both need God more than ever."

Antonne rubbed his face with both hands, "This is too much. I just got here you know!" He spoke emphatically and threw both hands into the air.

"I know. I'm sorry about that. But I'm leaving the day after tomorrow, and God said leap. So, I did."

"I can't believe this is happening right now." Antonne stared out the window by their booth. "You know I'll be there.

Of course, I'll be there. I probably won't be any help, but I'll be there. And, boy, you better pray hard that God decides to let me in on the plan if I'm supposed to do somethin', because otherwise, we're all in big trouble."

"Don't worry, God always does His part. The tricky part is making sure we do ours."

CHAPTER SEVEN

Beau gritted his teeth against the strain in his shoulder as he pulled back against the bright green resistance band his physical therapist had set up for him to use as his final exercise of the day. He felt stiff and uncomfortable. Pain moved up and down his right arm and into his neck. Every movement felt like a fight. Beau felt as though his body had betrayed him. One day shy of turning 21 years old and he felt trapped by his own skin. He clenched his jaw, becoming frustrated, and with a few final reps, he attempted to force his shoulder to comply with his mind. He looked forward to some time in the hot tub and the session he would have with his massage therapist later in the afternoon. As he wrapped up his exercise, his physical therapist called him over to an exam table.

Beau climbed up onto the table and scooted back enough to allow his feet to dangle freely above the floor. He looked down at his double-knotted sneakers and tried not to think about the ache in his shoulder. As his therapist walked over, Beau made a mental note of the man's height and stature. It seemed almost comical that this tall, unusually thin man was an authority in physical development. His therapist pulled a stool over next to the exam table and took a seat. The stool sat lower than the table itself, and though the man was tall, he was forced to look up to make eye contact with Beau. He adjusted the glasses on the bridge of his nose and cleared his throat, "How we feeling today?"

"Not bad, but not good either," Beau let out an abrupt half laugh and shrugged.

"How are you feeling about the progress you've made so far?" His therapist stood to his feet as he spoke and proceeded to place his hands on Beau's shoulder. As he palpated and pushed against the tissue, he noted both swelling and tension. Beau instinctively leaned his head slightly toward his left shoulder. This routine was old hat.

"To be honest, I don't really know. I think I can tell I'm getting better. But I can't seem to do all the things I want to do. And I really feel like I get the most relief from massage therapy. I'm usually good for the rest of the day, or as good as I can be, but then the next day it hurts like h..." he stopped himself. "It really hurts. I'm stiffer the day after massage therapy than usual, but it still feels like it helps more than anything else somehow."

"Okay. Well. I'm glad that you're noticing the improvement. On paper, you are, in fact, showing improvement, slight improvement. But I have to be honest, you're not making the kind of progress I had hoped for. I think most of that stems from scar tissue. And that's likely the reason you feel the most relief after massage therapy." He took a breath and continued, "Your manual therapist really digs into the scar tissue and that probably provides you with some added mobility for a while. But then, your body does what our bodies are designed to do and develops inflammation in response to the, for lack of a better word, trauma of the massage therapy itself."

"And that means," Beau hesitated for a moment, trying to put his finger on what his therapist was trying to say without becoming condescending. "What exactly?"

"Well, I'm afraid it means that you're still going to need that surgery. I mean, it's not my call to make. Your doctor needs to do that, but I have to send my report to Dr. Daniels later this week. And, based on your numbers, you're definitely not ready to be released. You still have a long way to go to regain full mobility in that shoulder, and I just don't see it happening without the surgery." The therapist took a deep breath and let it out slowly. Beau had made no secret of the fact that he was not interested in having surgery again. And he also knew that Beau was anxious to go back to full active duty as a Marine. "I know it's not what you want to hear, but it would be a disservice to you for me to say you're ready when you're not." He stepped away from Beau and sat back down on his stool. He looked up at him, as if waiting for him to say something.

Beau nodded. A look of unwilling defeat fell across his face and there was no hiding his disappointment. He didn't have anything to say, nor did he feel like saying anything. He wiped his forehead with his fingers, hard, in an attempt to keep back the heat of anger he could feel rising from his stomach and spreading into his face. It was like someone had turned on an oven inside his body. He couldn't help himself, he deeply resented his therapist. Beau's knee-jerk reaction was to blame him, but logic won out over his irrational thoughts. He wanted to scream, but instead he sighed. He knew it wasn't his therapist's fault. He knew it wasn't Dr. Daniels fault. And he tried his best to convince himself that it wasn't his fault either — but that effort was of little comfort to him, especially as he was overwhelmed by an uncontrollable feeling of rage bubbling in the pit of his belly. His anger was directed at no one in particular, but it was menacing all the same. And all he could do to prevent himself from lashing out was to grit his teeth, hard. His jaw was so tight his therapist could see the tension in his cheeks.

"I'll leave you to it now. Twenty minutes in the hot tub, and then you'll go see Caroline in the massage suite." As he stood, he laid a hand on Beau's shoulder — a consolation prize for the hard work that had fallen short. As soon as the therapist walked away, Beau began to place blame, not on the therapist, but on himself. He wondered if maybe he had just worked harder, or stretched more, or pretended that things didn't hurt even when they did, that maybe it wouldn't have come to this. He had held out hope that he wouldn't need the surgery at all, even though Dr. Daniels seemed fairly certain he would. Now that it seemed his hope had been fruitless, he also felt a certain amount of fear. Not fear of the surgery, but of what having an additional surgery might mean for his career with the Marines. It seemed almost cruel that the surgery he needed in order to do his job effectively could be the very thing that would end his career.

He stood up from his seat on the exam table and turned to make his way toward the locker room. As he changed, he reached into his bag and pulled out his bottle of painkillers. He shook the orange plastic cylinder between his large fingers, there weren't many pills left. He knew it wasn't time for a refill, but he also knew that one pill wouldn't do it — maybe not even two. For a moment, he felt guilt. He had tried to promise himself that he was done, and in a way, he had promised Andy too. But then he felt a familiar ache forming in his body, like every nerve ending was standing on edge. He physically could not stop himself from opening the bottle and swallowing two pills. He finished getting dressed and walked over to the sink. He splashed some water on his face and, as he stared at his own reflection, he told himself that tomorrow would be a better day to stop. He let himself feel comforted by the fact that his troubles would soon seem far away, at least for a little while. He made his way through the gym and into the pool area. There were only a few people in the water, working on some resistance therapy, and there was nobody in the hot tub. He breathed a sigh of relief under his breath and walked over to the welcoming bubbles.

~

The drive home felt surreal. As Beau drove, he moved his right shoulder as much as he could. Today's massage therapy session had been especially intense, but with that intensity came freedom. Beau knew it wouldn't last long, and part of his relief was likely the pain pills, but he welcomed the ability to roll his shoulder and to rest his arm across the back of the passenger seat in his truck. It wasn't much, but on a typical day, raising his arm that way would've been excruciating. As he drove, though, he found himself dwelling on the idea of another surgery, more recovery time, more reasons for the Marine Corps to send him packing. He willed himself to shake these dark thoughts from his mind and decided that he wouldn't tell anyone about the therapist's recommendation, at least not today. Andy's leave would end in a couple of days, and he thought it might be better to wait until he saw Dr. Daniels face-to-face before he told everyone he would have to go back under the knife.

As he pulled into the driveway, he realized that he didn't remember half of the drive home. He tried not to let that thought bother him, it wasn't the first time he had lost hours to a pill bottle. He noticed that Andy's truck was still gone. That meant Andy was still out, trying his best to teach Antonne about a town he knew almost nothing about himself. As he slid out of the truck, he moved unsteadily up the sidewalk, fumbling for his house key. He paused for a moment on the front steps and looked around the yard, absently taking in the warmth of the sun on his face. Briefly, he thought about Andy and how much he would miss him when he left, but he pushed that thought out of his mind. He didn't want to think. He didn't want to feel. Not today. All he really wanted to do was sleep.

CHAPTER EIGHT

Valerie sat quietly at the kitchen table, her Bible open in front of her, but she found it hard to focus. She was so excited about celebrating the twins twenty-first birthday, she could hardly think of anything else. She found herself overjoyed at the fact that both of her boys were alive and well, because for so long it hadn't look like they'd ever make it to this point. She closed her eyes and thanked God for Eli's miraculous healing and for Beau's saved life. She found herself so overcome with gratitude that the tears rolled down her cheeks and dripped on the thin pages of the Bible that rested on the table in front of her.

She hadn't told Beau or Eli, but she'd spent several weeks planning a catered event that would take place in the backyard the following afternoon. She had been doing her best to find ways to get the boys out of the house the next morning.

And Joe had promised to ask them to join him at the golf course. Andy, Antonne and Julia were in on the surprise and had promised to help decorate and get things set up. She had invited everyone who she could think of, even the boys' doctors. She knew they probably wouldn't come, but the fact that they'd played such a major role in everyone's lives over the last three years, this last year in particular, it seemed wrong not to ask them to come and celebrate the lives of two young men who almost didn't live to see their twenty-first birthday. In her mind, this birthday party would be the biggest birthday party her sons had ever had. She'd secretly been cleaning every corner of the house all week, almost every minute of every day had been filled with preparation. She hoped it would be the surprise of a lifetime.

Joe snuck in quietly behind her, placing his hands gently on her shoulders. She looked up at him and smiled, and he could see the tears in her eyes. "What's wrong?" he asked. He pulled out a chair and sat next to her, concern evident in his voice.

"Nothing!" Valerie said, laughing. "These are happy tears! Our babies turn twenty-one tomorrow. Can you believe it? Can you believe we made it here? I was just sitting here thanking God for what we have because things could've looked so much different right now. If He hadn't taken care of us, if He hadn't taken care of our boys, we wouldn't be celebrating this day, we would be grieving it. So now, I can't get over how far we've come and how grateful I am for the opportunity to celebrate a day we didn't know we'd ever see."

Joe smiled. He leaned over and kissed Val gently on the forehead. "I know exactly what you mean. I was thinking about that last night. I was talking with Bill Miller on the phone, and he reminded me that it was three years ago that very day that they dedicated an entire men's group at church to praying for our boys. Since then, they've met every week to pray for our boys... Imagine that. They're still meeting too. And they're still praying for Beau and Eli, specifically for Beau and Eli, and a few others now I'm sure — after all, they've seen their prayers answered, just like us. Now they've got a taste of the good life!" He laughed and put an arm around his wife. "So tell me about tomorrow. What should I expect?"

Valerie spent the next twenty-five minutes explaining the ins and outs of her plan. She explained to Joe that nothing would work if he didn't manage to get the boys out of the house and to the golf course early in the morning. Joe planned to make it a mandatory birthday father-and-son morning. His plan was to tell them that he wanted them to be together that day because it was a rite of passage, and he wanted to spend some time with them and talk to them about grown men things.

"Grown men things?" Valerie chuckled. "You might want to think of a better way to put it than that."

"What? You don't think that sounds enticing? Doesn't make you want to rush right out and spend time with me?" He laughed at his own words.

"Well, you make it sound like you're going to talk to them about IRAs and, you know, taxes or something." She laughed out loud and gave Joe a playful jab to his shoulder.

"Fine, fine. I'll come up with something that sounds more fun. But, since I'm making it mandatory, I could make it sound like a root canal and they'd still have to come."

~

Beau felt incredibly groggy when he woke up from his nap. He stretched and fumbled around on the bedside table to find his phone. It was six o'clock in the evening. He blinked his eyes hard against the light of his phone and waited for his brain to catch up with his wakefulness. Why hadn't anyone come to get him up? It was dinner time already. He sat up on the edge of the bed and rubbed his face with his hands. He reached for the water bottle on his bedside table and took a sip. His shoulder was already beginning to feel stiff, and he regretted wasting the relief of his massage on a nap. He stood to his feet, stretched again and made his way toward the door. When he opened the door, he could smell dinner wafting up the stairs. He could hear the television and the sounds of voices, and in a subtle way, the evidence of his family made him feel comforted. He turned to move toward the stairs, and as he walked, he looked down over the landing into the great room. Antonne and Andy were on the couch, Julia was in the recliner holding the baby, the TV was tuned to ESPN and, as he turned at the top of the stairs, he could see his father in the kitchen setting the table. He could hear his mother singing, and his dad would join in every few stanzas. The house smelled wonderful, and as Beau took in everything that was happening around him, a familiar stab of guilt bubbled up in his heart.

"Well, hello there sleepyhead!" Julia was smiling as she spoke. "You slept almost as long as your son today."

"Yeah," Beau said. "Therapy really wore me out today."

"We haven't been back long ourselves," Andy added.

"Yeah, and he here helped me be lost all over Longview today," Antonne said and laughed at his own joke. Andy made a face.

"Hardy har har," Andy said jeeringly.

Beau walked through the great room and into the kitchen. Eli was buttering rolls and Val was pulling something out of the oven. "Hi honey! Val said. "We thought you might stay in bed for the rest of the night. I peeked in at you to see if you wanted a snack, but you were out. I decided not to wake you."

"Thanks, mom," Beau said, his voice still gruff with sleep.

"Oh good," Eli feigned excitement. "Now that you're here, perhaps you can do something useful to help with dinner," he said mockingly, his words laced with sarcasm.

"No thanks," Beau said. "I feel like I'm pretty busy right now." His comeback was so dry and perfect that Eli had to laugh.

"Seriously though, Beau," Valerie chimed in, "there's a stack of towels on the dryer in the laundry room. Would you mind carrying them down to Antonne's bathroom please?"

Beau sighed, "Sure." As he walked, he thought about how strange it sounded for his mom to call the basement bathroom Antonne's bathroom. He wondered how long it would take him to get used to the idea of having Antonne around all the time. He walked into the laundry room and then made his way down a short hallway and through the basement door. There was a lamp on downstairs, and he navigated the stairs easily. He turned the corner into the bathroom and flipped on the light. As he placed the towels on the countertop, he noticed Antonne's toiletries bag open beside the sink. For a second, he wondered if Antonne planned to unpack it at all or if it hadn't quite hit him that this was his home now. He felt his breath catching in his chest when he noticed two orange pill bottles inside the toiletries bag nestled between a small can of shaving cream and a stick of deodorant.

Beau stood, frozen. For a split second his mind registered the reason Antonne had been discharged from the Army. He had suffered damage to both legs and had gone through extensive surgery. It stood to reason that he would have some ongoing medical needs. Beau felt his heart beating harder inside his chest. Instinctively, he turned to look out the bathroom door and into the basement. What was he thinking? He couldn't do this. This was wrong. But after ensuring that the coast was clear, he closed the door and locked it. He couldn't seem to help himself. He turned on the water, and then, as quietly as he could, he reached into Antonne's bag and pulled out the pill bottles. He turned them over in his hands to inspect the labels. One of the bottles was nearly full, and one had clearly been used but still had a number of pills inside. The used bottle contained a sixty-day supply of 800 mg ibuprofen. The other bottle said oxycodone and acetaminophen. Beau left the water running, placed the ibuprofen back on the counter and cleared his throat as he opened the second bottle. He took a few strides toward the toilet and pushed the lever down to flush it in an effort to mask the sound of the pills leaving the bottle as he shook several into his hand. He was careful not to take too many, he didn't want them to be missed. When he was satisfied with the number of pills he would keep versus the number of pills remaining in the bottle, he carefully replaced the lid and slipped his handful of pills into his pocket. He carefully positioned the bottles as they had been before. He couldn't remember exactly how the labels were turned, so he left them at different angles, each facing away from the top of the bag. When he was finished, he rinsed his hands under the running water and dried them on the towel hanging by the sink. He unlocked the door and slowly opened it, peeking out into the hallway and the open space in the basement living area. Nobody. He made his way across the room and climbed back up the stairs. He felt a rush of adrenaline and nervousness as he walked into the kitchen. How long had he been downstairs? It felt like he was in the bathroom for a long time. Had anyone noticed? He waited for someone to say something, but no one did. So, he just stood in the kitchen — trying to act normal.

After a few minutes, Julia came walking through the door of the kitchen from the great room. She was holding baby Gabe over one shoulder and patting his back. Beau took one look at the two of them together and felt a little sick to his stomach. But he decided that he was doing what he had to do.

He walked over to Julia and placed his hand on Gabe's back. "Gaby, my baby," he said as he lifted Gabe from Julia's shoulder. He cradled the baby in his arms and kissed his tiny head. Julia smiled as she watched them together. "I'm just gonna go sit in here for a little while," Beau announced as he carried the baby out of the kitchen and back into the great room.

Once Beau was comfortably seated in the recliner, Julia looked around the kitchen. "What can I do to help?" she asked no one in particular. As she moved toward Eli, she could feel an unfamiliar tension forming between them. He smiled at her weakly as he looked up at her from his position at the counter, she smiled back. She wondered if things between them would ever be the same.

"Honestly, I think we've about got it wrapped up here. We'll probably be ready to eat in about ten or fifteen minutes," Val said, her words were almost a song. Joy poured out of her voice and filled the room. "Eli has just been a dinnertime dynamo today!"

"Yeah, you go rest," Eli said as he set the timer on the oven to brown the rolls.

"Let's both go rest, milady," Joe interjected, as he took a deep bow and extended an elbow toward Julia.

"Well, don't mind if I do," Julia sang back as she took Joe's arm. "I do declare," she fanned as the two strode through the kitchen and into the great room. Eli walked over and placed some trivets on the kitchen table. It was easier to keep busy than it was to be around Julia — especially when Julia was around Beau. He glanced up and saw Julia sitting on the arm of the recliner, stroking the back of Beau's head with her hand. He told himself to look away, but he couldn't. And when Julia looked up and caught him staring, he saw what looked like pain in her face. He wished she hadn't caught him, because her pain was the last thing he wanted to see.

CHAPTER NINE

"Happy birthday to you, happy birthday to you, happy birthday dear Beau and Eli, happy birthday to you!" Joe, Valerie, Julia, Andy, and Antonne sang in unison over two stacks of incredibly large Belgian waffles covered in whipped cream and tiny chocolate chips. The breakfast restaurant they had frequented for years pulled out all the stops to help celebrate Beau and Eli's twenty-first birthday. Everyone was in good spirits, including Beau. Valerie checked her watch several times, she knew that the company she hired to set up the DJ booth in the backyard would be arriving any minute. So far, things were working out perfectly. Joe would take both boys to the golf course, and everyone else would head back to the house to get ready for the big night. Everyone ate, sipped coffee, and chatted as waitstaff and other breakfast patrons gushed over baby Gabe's infectious behavior and cherub-like features.

"Well, I think it's safe to say that today is a very good day," Joe piped up. He placed his arm over the back of Valerie's chair and smiled his broadest McKnight smile. "We're going to have to head out soon if we want to make our tee time." When he spoke, Beau looked at Julia. Only she had heard his opinion of the golf outing. What good is golf to a man who can't move his shoulder? He didn't say a word though, and Julia smiled at him reassuringly. "But first, your mother and I have a surprise for you." He stretched and tried to act nonchalant. Meanwhile, Valerie was beaming. It was clear she was about to bust from excitement. The anticipation seemed to be affecting Julia, Andy, and Antonne just as much as it was Beau and Eli.

"Well?" Eli asked, making a face that caused the whole table to burst into laughter.

Joe cleared his throat before continuing, clearly dragging the moment out for dramatic effect, "The last few years have been, well, pretty big. And we decided that it was high time we put the hard times behind us and moved on to a new chapter. So, to set some things right and back to normal, we've made arrangements for each of you to have a new truck." Julia squealed and Eli fell back in his chair and looked up at the ceiling. He hadn't seen his truck after the accident, but he had seen pictures. Totaled was an understatement. Beau's truck had also been totaled and, when he got to Lejeune, he'd purchased a beat-up old truck that he hadn't seen since before he left for Afghanistan. He doubted it would still run. Since Joe and Valerie had been under the financial strain of legal matters and medical bills, new vehicles simply hadn't been an option, until now. Both boys had been borrowing their dad's truck or mom's SUV to get around town, or just catching rides. A couple times, when Julia had been unable to drive him, Beau had been forced to take his dad's company car to his therapy appointment. It was a huge no-no, but Joe had said that drastic times called for drastic measures. He'd sent Beau to the appointment, and then retrospectively cleared the situation with his company. Beau distinctively remembered his dad saying that he normally wouldn't advocate for the "ask forgiveness later" philosophy, but that sometimes exceptions had to be made. Beau covered his mouth with his hand. Feelings of both excitement and guilt battled for space in his brain.

"Now, you need to know that we won't be buying them brand-new. That's just not in the financial cards right now. But, we figured we could go tomorrow after we get Andy to the airport."

"I don't know what to say! Thank you! Thank you so much!" Eli said, his voice filled with eager anticipation that reminded Valerie of his childlike excitement on Christmas Eve. She smiled, silently thankful that they'd be able to make it work financially. She had agreed to step in as part of the church office staff until a replacement could be found for Susan, the front office secretary. Susan's husband had retired and, even though she hadn't intended on retiring at the same time, he was eager to travel and get into missions and she wanted to accompany him. So, her slightly early retirement left room for Valerie to work part time. The plan was for her to put this income toward the new vehicles. She was excited to be a part of the process and, strangely, just as excited to be joining the workforce again — albeit temporarily.

Beau found himself speechless. He wasn't sure how to process the tumultuous feelings swirling around in his gut. He was the reason they needed new trucks to begin with. He was the reason the past few years had been so hard. And even now, he was hiding a dark secret from his family. He didn't deserve his parent's mercy. He didn't deserve their blessings. In his mind, he was irredeemable — but somehow, Joe and Valerie loved him with an unconditional and giving love and he didn't know why. At that moment, he happened to look over at his son, and it suddenly clicked. He knew the reason. He now knew why. He knew, without a doubt, that no behavior in Gabe's future could negate the love he had for his son. He turned and looked at Julia, who was giddy with excitement. For the past few weeks, she had bubbled over with joy everywhere she went. It was attractive, but somehow irritating at the same time. But he knew that her love for their son was unconditional as well. He reached across the table and grabbed his mom's hand and squeezed it. "Thanks, guys," he said with heartfelt gratitude.

Beau looked at Julia, who added, "This is huge! You have no idea what a difference this will make!" She looked back at Joe and Valerie and continued, "We were literally just having this conversation. My car needs tires, brakes... My car basically needs a new car!" She laughed and then added, "And depending on what happens with Beau's medical board, paying to fix my car and to try and get Beau something to drive was just going to cost so much... You guys are the best!" She was so excited that her words came out in peppered bursts that made Joe smile.

"It's our pleasure. We're just happy that we're able to do it." He turned and looked at Val and pushed her hair back from her shoulder. "Hon, can you handle the check? I gotta get these boys to the golf course or we'll be late for our tee time."

"Of course!" She leaned over and kissed her husband tenderly, then she stood up and opened her arms, wiggling her fingers as she always did when she expected her boys to offer up massive hugs. After hugs and love had been passed all around, Joe and the boys left the restaurant and made their way toward Joe's truck. Valerie took care of the check, including Andy's and Antonne's.

"You don't have to do that Mrs. V!" Antonne piped up. "I don't have a lot of money, but I've got enough to buy my breakfast," he said, laughingly.

"So do I!" Andy added.

"Well I don't," Julia sighed and belly laughed after the words passed her lips. Valerie started laughing too and Andy just shook his head.

"Nonsense!" Valerie said. "What mama doesn't want to spoil her kids when she can?"

Antonne set up a little straighter. He instantly felt a sense of pride and belonging he hadn't known in his whole life. His family life as a young man had been so difficult that the Army had become his family. Without the Army, he was afraid he might never belong anywhere again. But the McKnight's had changed all that. For a brief second, he thought about the fact that everything that had happened to the McKnight family had resulted in his becoming one of them. If Eli had never gotten hurt, Beau would've never joined the Marines. If Beau hadn't joined the Marines, he would never have met Andy, he wouldn't have been injured in Afghanistan, he wouldn't have ended up in that hospital bed and Antonne would've never known he existed. For that matter, if he had never broken his legs or ended up getting medically discharged, these people he now loved so dearly would never have become part of his life. He felt himself getting emotional as he remembered something that Andy had said the day he learned about Beau's addiction. "God doesn't make the bad things happen, but He can use the bad things and turn them into good things. All we have to do is trust Him to turn our ashes into beauty."

"How about we just leave the tip then?" Andy asked as he reached into his back pocket to retrieve his wallet. "At least let me do that."

"Yeah! I want in on this." Antonne reached into his pocket.

"I've got an idea," Andy said. "What if we pay it forward and give this waitress what we would've paid if Ms. Val wasn't buying our breakfast?"

"I'm down with that!" Antonne replied, enthusiastically. "Boy, I like the way you think." As he spoke, he slapped cash down onto the table with a flourish.

"No fair!" Julia said. "I only have a five."

"I'm sure she won't mind," Andy replied with a laugh.

"You kids are absolutely the best! I just love this. Y'all are going to make me cry!" Valerie said.

"Don't cry, Mrs. V!" Antonne said. He walked around to the side of the table where Valerie sat and sang, "Let's get this party started!" He began to dance as he continued to sing to his own beat. Valerie started to laugh. Antonne was so infectious. She stood up, and when she did, Antonne stood beside her, urging her to throw out her own dance moves. "Come on Mrs. V, get some!" he grunted and laughed as he moved his head from one side to the other. Julia and Andy were both laughing. They didn't expect Valerie to join in, but she did. The tables in their general vicinity all got a laugh out of the spectacle. "Dang!" Antonne stretched the word out for added emphasis. "Mrs. V got moves! For real though — moves!"

Valerie laughed, and as they walked through the door, she reached to take the diaper bag from Julia. She then turned and looked at all of them and, with a straight face, said "We will never speak of this again." They were still laughing as they climbed into Valerie's SUV. It was obvious that the day's plan was falling into place perfectly.

CHAPTER TEN

"Breathe it in boys!" Joe said, as they walked around to the backside of the clubhouse where they would retrieve their golf carts. "Who's toting who?" Joe asked. "I'm not opposed to you two birthday boys riding together, if you want. It won't hurt my feelings."

"What does it matter? Y'all both know I'm not going to be able to swing a club. I will be useless! Why am I even here?" Beau said with bitterness in his voice. He had avoided the topic since the day Joe brought up the golf course. It was something they had done together for years and Beau knew his dad was just trying to make things nostalgic for their birthday. But when he stepped out of the clubhouse, resentment hit him in the face. He couldn't do what he used to do and that made him feel both angry and helpless.

Eli couldn't help it. He was still upset with Beau. No matter how hard he tried, he couldn't get over the fact that his brother — whom he'd always admired in a weird kind of way — had given control of his life to a pill, a pill that could also claim his life. He had tried to let it go, but in his heart, he knew that Beau had not been true to his word. No matter what Beau said, Eli did not believe he would be able to walk away from his issue. His attitude at the moment wasn't helping either, so Eli decided to compensate for Beau's mood with his own enthusiasm. "How about we take turns? That way, nobody is driving alone the whole time."

"Great idea!" Joe said. He chose to ignore Beau's outburst and proceeded to strap his clubs into the back of the golf cart. Eli glanced in Beau's direction before placing his own clubs in the back of the cart next to his father's.

Beau had been able to feel the mounting tension between him and Eli since the day Gabe was born. Knowing that Eli had been there with Andy that night and how scared and hurt he had been added an extra dimension to the guilt that Beau already felt. He couldn't help but wonder if Eli secretly blamed him for what had happened graduation night. He wondered if Eli harbored untold resentment against him because of the coma. He wondered how anybody could be that forgiving and how anybody who had been through what Eli had been through could be so peaceful and joyful all the time. Even knowing there was tension between them, Beau couldn't help but be slightly envious of his brother's outlook on life.

Beau quietly carried his clubs to the other cart and placed them in the back. He took one set of keys from his father and told them that he needed to go to the restroom and would meet them on the first green. Eli glared at him. He couldn't help but be suspicious of Beau's every move, despite Andy's reassurance that Beau was making an effort. His expression was not lost on Beau. He and his twin had always had a deep connection and it seemed to Beau that he could almost feel his brother's suspicion.

"Sounds good, son!" Joe exclaimed. He was in a great mood. He hopped in the cart and patted the seat beside him, signaling Eli to sit down. He glanced at his watch. "We actually have some time for some warm up balls. Meet us over at the driving range."

"Okay," Beau said, turning on his heel and making his way to the clubhouse. He adjusted his visor and dropped the set of golf cart keys into his pocket. He made his way through the clubhouse to the restrooms. Once safely inside the men's room, he found a stall and reached into his other pocket. He held three pills in the palm of his hand and debated whether or not he should try taking just one. He needed three, but he didn't want to need them at all, so maybe he could take just one and be okay. But he didn't have that willpower, so he made a mental compromise and dropped one pill back into his pocket and threw two into his mouth. After he was finished in the restroom, he washed his face and hands and tried to convince himself that he didn't have a problem.

~

At the ninth hole, Joe, Eli and even Beau, to his surprise, were all playing fairly well. None of them were exceptional golfers, but they were all talented enough to hold their own and enjoy the game. Joe had always loved golf and had raised his boys to swing a club since they were about four years old. "How about a little snack?" Joe pulled his car off the path and drove toward the ninth hole snack shack. Eli and Beau had been taking turns driving the second cart after every two holes.

As Eli followed his dad and brother toward the snack shack, he wondered if he should confront Beau about his issue. Except, when he thought about it, he also thought about the secret he was keeping — his unexpected and unrequited love for Julia — and he felt like a hypocrite. But, ultimately, he decided that the main difference between his secret and his brother's secret was that Beau's was potentially deadly. As they pulled in the lot to park, Eli had almost decided he was going to confront Beau in front of their dad. But, as he had always covered for Beau in the past, he just couldn't make himself do that to his brother. He decided it would be best to confront Beau alone first and get all his suspicions and concerns out in the open before going to his parents. He wondered what Julia would say. He wondered if it would change how she felt about Beau. He wondered if it would be a window of opportunity for him, but he quickly shook that thought from his mind, chastising his own soul for thinking it at all. He loved Beau. He couldn't imagine hurting him, no matter how he felt about Julia. His heart and his mind tore at each other like clawed beasts in a battle between good and evil.

They walked into the snack shack and took a seat at one of the small bistro tables. They ordered three hotdogs and a large fry to share. The fry orders at the snack shack were huge and not even one of the McKnight men attempted to single-handedly eat an order by himself. They sat eating, talking, and drinking water when Joe excused himself from the table and walked up to the counter. When he walked back to the table, he had three open bottles of beer between his fingers. Eli's eyes grew wide. He couldn't believe what he was seeing. Beau glanced in Eli's direction and raised his eyebrows. They could not hide the moment of shock they were sharing. "Um, what's up, Dad?" Eli asked, his voice slow, strange sounding, and filled with confusion.

"You're twenty-one years old today. And I wanted to buy you your first legal beer," Joe said. He had more to say, but before he could get his next sentence out, Eli chimed in, "Try first beer, ever." His mouth was hanging open. He felt like a little kid playing grown-up. Beau rolled his eyes at his brother's statement, because even if Eli didn't intend it to be, he knew it was a subtle dig at his expense.

Joe released a half chuckle before he continued, "But before we do this, I want to talk to you about something." He placed a bottle of beer in front of each of his sons and one next to his own plate. He slid his plate back a few inches and leaned forward to rest his elbows on the table. "In all the years of your lives, I've never been much of a drinker. And, as you know, I've never had a drink in front of you — ever. But, I will tell you that I occasionally have a beer or glass of scotch when I'm out with your mother or something like that. I want you to know that my choice not to drink isn't because I think it's inherently wrong. Yes, the Bible says drunkenness is a sin. I believe that. I believe that giving your self-control to anything is a sin. If you can't control your actions or your thoughts, the enemy will run roughshod over your life. Make no mistake, whether you're a redeemed man or not, if you willingly give yourself over to sin, you are opening the door for bad things to wreak havoc in your life.

But that's not what I want to talk to you about. And, it's not really the reason I have chosen not to drink. The truth is, many, many years ago when your mom and I were first married, I drank regularly. And I drank too much. When I turned twenty-one, I could buy it for myself — and I did. One time we were at the beach, some of our friends had gone too, and I drank so much that I was in and out of consciousness. Your mom was trying to help me get up a flight of stairs and I blacked out and fell. I pulled her down with me. We fell all the way down the stairs onto the concrete below. I only got a couple of small scrapes, but your mom was knocked unconscious. She had bruises all over her. Her chin was busted open. And I was so drunk that I didn't even know that it had happened until the next day when my friend told me he had driven my wife to the emergency room while I slept it off. I hated myself for it. Your mom knew it was an accident, but it was an accident that happened because of my choices. Now, I'm a believer. But when I was young, I had to learn things the hard way sometimes. That experience was definitely one of the harder lessons I've ever had to learn and I decided then and there that I would never, ever put myself in that situation again, because I never, ever wanted to hurt your mother again, physically or emotionally.

I know I was an embarrassment to her and I never wanted her to be embarrassed because of me again. The idea that I wasn't living up to the image of the man that I wanted to be or the man that she needed me to be was all I needed to change my ways. She could have died that day, and not only would it have been my fault, but I would've slept right through it. So, as we sip these beers and celebrate the rite of passage that is your twenty-first birthday, I want you to think about that, and I want to challenge you as men to make a commitment to yourselves and the people you love that you will never, ever give control of who you are to a substance that could claim your life or the life of someone you love. And that you will never, ever drink so much that it causes you to forget all about the man you want to be and the man that God expects you to be." Joe took his bottle and raised it to the center of the table. Beau and Eli looked at each other. Beau felt sick to his stomach. His palms were sweaty. Could he accept that challenge? He wanted to, but could he really? Neither he nor Eli had ever heard that story, nor would they have ever expected that something like that had happened to their father.

Eli reached for his bottle and raised it toward his father's, "I don't even think I want to try it now," he kind of chuckled to lighten the moment. "That was intense, Dad."

"It needed to be said. You didn't think I was going to bring you all the way out here on your birthday just to have a good time, did you?" Joe smiled.

Beau hesitantly reached for his bottle and raised it. The three men clinked their bottles together and then put them to their lips. For the first time ever, Beau took a small sip and placed the bottle back on the table, uncertain as to whether or not he planned to take a second. Joe swallowed his sip and placed his bottle back on the table, as well. Both Beau and Joe watched intently as Eli slowly registered the flavor of the beer on his tongue. He made a face that caused Joe to laugh. As he set the bottle back onto the table, he scrunched his nose and pulled his lips back to reveal all his front teeth, "That's awful!" He made a gagging sound. "Yuck! How in the world do people drink enough of this to become addicted to it?"

Joe laughed, "It is a bit of an acquired taste, so they say." He leaned over and put a hand on his son's shoulder. "Eli, my boy, not liking it is not a bad thing. But remember, not everything tastes like beer — and some stuff will hit you harder than beer ever dreamed about and go down without a fight. Be careful. Make good choices. Make Godly choices."

Joe looked at Beau through knowing eyes and smiled at him lovingly. Beau nodded. They didn't have to speak. Everyone at the table knew that Beau was no stranger to the flavor of beer and that his age had never stopped him. Joe leaned toward Beau and squeezed his left shoulder. "I love you. No matter what." He looked at Beau and then at Eli, "I love both of you. You make us very proud and I can't wait to see what God has in store for you both. Joe grabbed his bottle and made his way toward the door. Eli picked his up and followed behind him. Beau reached for his, as well — but, as his hand touched the cold glass, he suddenly felt empowered to walk away. He turned and made his way to the exit, leaving his full beer bottle on the table behind him as he focused on the man he wanted to be in the future.

CHAPTER ELEVEN

By three o'clock, the guys had just wrapped up their eighteenth hole. Across town, Valerie, Julia, Andy, and Antonne had everything set up and some of the guests were already beginning to arrive. Joe glanced at his watch. They were a few minutes ahead of schedule, so he suggested that they duck inside the clubhouse for a few minutes. Together, they browsed around the pro shop and both Beau and Eli expected they might get a birthday gift out of the deal, at least until Joe looked at his watch and abruptly decided it was time to head home.

"Okay, weirdo. That was the shortest shopping experience ever," Eli said, giving his dad a soft jab. Joe slid his phone out of his pocket and texted Valerie. It would take them about twenty minutes to get back to the house. Valerie was beside herself with excitement. She immediately began to run around telling all their guests that the birthday boys were on their way back. She had invited everyone she could think of. There were friends from church and friends from school, as well as family members and even friends of family.

Pete pulled in with Val's mom and dad in tow. Unfortunately, James and his family hadn't been able to make it. Joe's parents were in route, along with several other members of his family. The DJ had already begun playing music and Valerie took a few minutes to light some citronella candles on the banquet tables. There was food everywhere, with a single table dedicated to the birthday cake. Valerie hated the idea of bugs around the food, so there were tiki torches and citronella candles every few feet, and anything that could be covered with a lid was covered.

"I think it looks great Mrs. V!" Antonne seemed as excited as he would be if it were his party. It warmed Val's heart. He had spent the morning hanging streamers and paper decorations and she was so grateful for his help that she almost wished it was his birthday too. Valerie had decided against the paper lanterns because she knew that the kids had plans to go out in the evening, so Antonne suggested they put them on the tables as centerpieces instead. It looked fantastic, and he definitely succeeded in winning her over. She also decided on hanging an overabundance of balloons, which Andy and

Antonne had tied carefully to every surface they could find. Julia had cleaned every inch of every surface and had helped unload the folding chairs Val had borrowed from the church, strategically placing them all over the lawn. Now, everything was set, and they were ready.

Joe didn't say a word as he made that last familiar turn toward home. He let the car-lined street do the talking for him. Eli leaned forward in the backseat. "Dad?" he asked, with both excitement and confusion in his voice. "What's going on?"

"I dunno," Joe said. "We'll have to ask your mother."

"Right," Beau said sarcastically. "I'm sure you are completely clueless." Joe snickered with a knowing excitement as his boys became antsy.

Valerie knew that as soon as Joe turned onto their street, the boys would see all the cars lining the driveway and both sides of the road and the surprise would be out — but she would have loved to have seen their faces. Still, even knowing they'd have it figured out before she saw them, she was adamant that all the guests yell "Surprise!" anyway.

When Julia came sprinting around the side of the house yelling, "They're here! They're here," nearly fifty people waiting in the backyard drew quiet. The DJ prepared to blast a surprise-appropriate tune and everyone else watched the corner of the house intently.

Eli completely abandoned his golf clubs in the back of Joe's truck and made a beeline for the backyard. Beau was a little more hesitant. He paused as he stepped out of the truck, glancing around at the other vehicles nearby. Some of them he recognized, and some of them he didn't. Either way, he knew that he was likely going to come face-to-face with people he hadn't seen since before the accident. His guard came up instantly. However misplaced, he was feeling the sting of judgment even before he set foot on the lawn. But after he heard the loud, jubilant scream of "Surprise!" rising up over the roofline, he chose to confront his feelings head on.

He rounded the corner to hear a second wave of greetings. Julia ran up to give him a hug and Valerie followed close behind her carrying baby Gabe close to her body. Beau felt uncomfortable as he scanned the crowd of familiar faces. He saw some of his friends from high school, all who remembered the Beau he used to be. He wondered if, maybe, the only reason they showed up was to see the spectacle he had become. What if they didn't like him now? What if they felt sorry for him? He tried to shake these thoughts from his mind as one by one friends and family greeted him, hugged his neck, and did their best to make him feel loved.

Eli, on the other hand, was thrilled. He was so happy to see everyone. Through his eyes, everyone seemed to look different, because in his mind, far less time had passed than had passed for everyone else. He hugged everyone he came across and laughed and reminisced and was genuinely grateful to be alive. The only blip in his otherwise joyous experience came when Mr. Hinkley offered an inadvertent update on Ivy's work in the mission field. He eagerly told some of his old students about Ivy and Mark and how blessed they were in Zimbabwe, but he hadn't intended for Eli to hear it. It wasn't until he touched on the fact that they were considering coming back to the states together that Mr. Hinkley noticed Eli standing nearby. He quickly changed the subject, but the damage was already done. The smile slowly left Eli's face when he pictured Ivy and Mark together. And then when he looked across the lawn and saw Beau holding baby Gabe and Julia standing next to him, he felt an intense pang of jealousy. He cleared his throat and turned his back on everyone for a few moments. He then walked over to the buffet tables to load a plate with chicken strips and pasta salad.

Valerie, who could normally read her son like a book, simply assumed his heart was still scarred by Ivy. She wouldn't, in a million years, have guessed that hearing about Ivy and Mark was painful, but that it paled in comparison to the pain of unrequited love. If anything, she would have been shocked. Val walked over to Eli and adjusted his collar with her fingers, wanting to comfort him. "Happy birthday, sweet boy," she said as she pulled him closer to kiss his cheek.

"Thanks, Mom," Eli said. He balanced his plate in one hand, put his muscular arm around her shoulders, and gave her a squeeze.

Valerie grunted, "No one would ever guess that you were as soft as a noodle this time last year! You've nearly crushed my bones!" She laughed at her own words.

"Soft as a noodle?" Eli exclaimed, feigning exasperation. He gave his mom a light, playful shove to her shoulder. She heard Joe calling for her from across the yard and, as she walked away, she smacked Eli on his backside.

"You're never too old to whoop!" she called over her shoulder as she danced away. Eli smiled as he looked around the yard — so many people had come to celebrate their day, people he loved, but also people he felt like he didn't know anymore. In the corner of the yard, he saw his brother standing with some of their high school football friends and he wondered if, like him, Beau felt like a completely different person. Still, he was very grateful and, when he thought about his parent's generosity and all the people who loved him and how happy he was to be a part of little Gabe's life, he couldn't help but thank God for his blessings.

~

At about eight o'clock, the group of young people were standing around planning the night's festivities. Originally, Julia had hoped it would just be the five of them, but Beau seemed eager to celebrate with some of his old classmates. She recognized some of them from middle school and others were completely foreign to her. They all seemed like good guys, but Beau treated her differently — was somehow distant — in their presence. She wasn't sure how to take it but decided that his happiness on his birthday was more important to her than her own level of social comfort. She headed in through the sliding glass door to feed the baby and to chat with Valerie about the evening's plans. She had no doubts about Val's ability to take care of the baby, but she'd never left Gabe for more than an hour or so, and she felt a little guilty about leaving him behind. Val reassured her over and over again, so Julia finally made her way upstairs to freshen up.

Eli walked over to his group of old buddies and called out to Andy and Antonne to join their circle. He introduced each of them and they, in turn, were accepted into the fold. As they readied themselves to leave, Eli, Andy, and Antonne all began walking back to the house to say their goodbyes and grab their stuff. As they walked, Eli began to give them both a little run down on the characters who would join them for the night's festivities. He proceeded to explain how they were all good guys, each with his own brand of humor and attitude, but also with his own brand of issues. "Nick is the only one we need to keep an eye on. He and Beau have always had a love-hate relationship. And Heavy, Heavy could be trouble. Only because he drinks a lot, and Beau used to be his only challenger." Eli and Antonne chuckled, but Andy didn't laugh.

"I have a bad feeling about tonight," Andy said.

"Don't say that," Eli responded. "I mean, if any one of us should listen to his gut, it's you. But you know we're not bowing out of this, regardless."

"Yeah, you big killjoy," Antonne added. "Between ol' Hangdog and now Killjoy, we'll never have any fun around here," he laughed.

"I'm serious," Andy responded. "I feel it in my spirit." Antonne stopped laughing, and a serious look crossed his face. He pulled his eyebrows together and looked back and forth between Eli and Andy, as if searching for an answer to a question he didn't have to ask.

"Well, then that's all the more reason for us to be there. We know Beau's going, no matter what. And that means Julia's going. And if they're both going, we have to go. Who else will keep him straight?" Eli's voice was pleading. "We have to go."

Andy took a deep breath and then let it out slowly. "You're right. It will be better if we're there."

The birthday party lingered on, and all the guests continued to laugh and eat and catch up on things that had happened since they'd last been together, despite the fact that the guests of honor were ready to hit the town. A few of the boys' high school friends, and several of their girlfriends, congregated in the driveway waiting on what they were calling "go time." Sum total, the group stood at twelve. Joe, Valerie, and some of the other parents were giving adamant instructions about using good judgment and driving carefully — all the things one would expect from a parent under similar circumstances. The plan was for the group to head to a bar downtown, where they could play pool and dance. Julia, Andy, and one of the other girls had not yet turned twenty-one. So Julia chose a place that would allow them to enter and only required ID for drinks. The group planned to carpool and, once the decisions had been made about who would ride where and with whom, everyone said their goodbyes, Julia kissed Gabe at least twenty-five times, and they were off. Beau, Julia, Antonne, Andy, and Eli all squeezed into Julia's car because she was the only one who had a full tank of gas. As they drove, the conversation turned to Andy's imminent departure.

"What time do you have to be at the airport tomorrow?" Julia asked.

"Not until about three. My flight's not until five-thirty," Andy said calmly.

"What about your truck?" Eli asked. "I thought that was, you know, *your* truck."

"It is. My parents have been traveling the whole coast and they're in North Florida, maybe South Carolina by now. They're driving my mom's little car and will come to meet me in North Carolina. They'll leave me the car, then they'll fly out here and take my truck back home. It seemed to make more sense than all of us driving cross country in opposite directions."

"I can't believe you have to go," Julia said, pouting. "It's going to be weird here without you."

"Believe it or not, I don't want to go. But I don't have a long time left on my enlistment, so, who knows? I'll probably have one more deployment before I can escape though," Andy laughed. He knew God had called him to the Marines, but he certainly didn't hear God calling him to stay.

"Beau, does that mean there's just a year or so left on your enlistment too?" Julia asked.

"That's what it means. Not that it will matter. I'll go have this…" Beau caught himself. He almost mentioned the scar tissue surgery, but he wasn't ready to tell anyone.

"You'll go have what?" Julia asked.

"Nothing. Never mind." Beau didn't want to think about the Marine Corp. All he'd wanted for so long was to get back to work, and now he was beginning to believe it would never happen. He squeezed the steering wheel of Julia's car until his knuckles turned white. He felt a familiar heat in his face and took a deep breath. "Let's talk about *anything* else," he said curtly. His resentful tension infected the whole car. No one wanted to talk after that and the remainder of the drive was spent in near silence.

CHAPTER TWELVE

The first hour of the night had been great. Everyone was having a good time. The group laughed and played pool and danced, and even Andy seemed to be having a good time — though the bar scene was definitely *not* his scene. Beau excused himself to go to the restroom and, as had become his custom, he reached into his pocket to retrieve a couple of pills. He was already out of his own prescription, and his appointment with his doctor was still days away. He fumbled in his pocket for the first of the pills he'd stolen from Antonne's bag. He'd had just enough to drink that not even the guilt slowed him down this time.

Beau and Eli's group of buddies were, one by one, ordering drinks. As a result, there was no shortage of alcohol at their table. Beau had already downed two beers when one of his friends ordered a round of shots. Eli had been holding onto the same beer for the full hour, hoping no one would notice that he wasn't drinking it. He'd spent the bulk of his night shooting pool with Antonne, who had surprised them all with his skills.

"When I was growin' up, the basketball courts at the youth center were almost always reserved, and I had to do something with my time, so I did this," he said, as he banked a shot to win yet another game against Eli. Andy sat at a nearby table drinking water and eating a basket of wings he'd ordered at the bar. He quietly observed all that was going on around him, and to his surprise, he was enjoying himself. Julia was sipping on plain club soda and had been getting to know some of the other girls. She seemed to be having a good time and had been all too happy to show the other girls pictures of Gabe. They had, of course, gushed over his round, dimpled cheeks and big blue eyes and, by all accounts, she seemed happy.

Eli walked over to Andy and nodded in Beau's direction. "I think he's had two shots already and two beers, and we've only been here an hour," Eli whispered somewhat loudly so Andy could hear him. He put special emphasis on the words *an hour.* Andy simply nodded and continued to watch the room. He could feel Eli's concern, and he had to admit, he had concerns of his own. Within what seemed like mere minutes, Beau had gone from laughing with his old friends and dancing with Julia to slurring his words and making cruel jokes at the expense of whoever happened to be standing nearby. Eli proved an easy target, and not even Julia was off limits. The only person who couldn't tell that Beau had reached his limit was Beau himself. He reached into the ice bucket full of beer on the middle of the table and pulled out another drink. He could barely stand on his own two feet, and Eli became suspicious, thinking that his rapid decline wasn't the result of alcohol alone. Andy stood up to walk over to Beau, but Eli stopped him. Antonne was standing nearby and stepped closer to hear what Eli had to say. "I think he's pilled up too. I'd put money on it," Eli said. He gritted his teeth and shook his head, obviously frustrated.

"That's what I'm afraid of too," Andy said. He looked at Antonne, reminding him of the conversation they'd shared earlier in the week. He then looked back at Eli and added, "Mixing booze and pills like that could kill him."

Eli nodded. He looked over his shoulder at Antonne. "I think we need to get him home," Eli said worriedly. Antonne nodded his agreement.

A couple of Beau's other friends had already had enough of Beau's drunken behavior, but both Nick and Heavy were egging him on. "I've never seen anyone get so drunk, so fast, McKnight." Nick gave Beau a shove to his shoulder and laughed at his own words.

Heavy slapped Beau on the back and added, "Well, he's just getting started, ain't you McKnight?" Heavy was as heavy as ever and, having always had a likeness for beer, it was no surprise he seemed completely sober despite the amount of alcohol he'd consumed since they'd arrived.

Julia was starting to become uncomfortable. She could tell something wasn't right, and it didn't just seem like alcohol. She knew Beau and, even though he hadn't been the same in a long time and he slept a lot more than he used to, this behavior was strange, even for him. As Eli got closer, she stood up and took a step toward him. "I don't like him this way," she said. "He's kind of mean." Her nearness caused Eli's heart to beat faster and he tensed up. When she sensed his uneasiness, she took a step back. She looked down at her feet and then back up at Eli. He had Beau's face, but he definitely wasn't Beau, though for a split second, she almost wished he was — she almost wished the tables were turned. Abruptly, she stopped that train of thought, chastising herself for even entertaining such an idea.

She began to feel a little uncertain. What if Beau never became the Beau she remembered? What if she had let herself fall in love with the Beau of her past and who he used be, instead of the man he was now? She had expected Eli's miracle to relieve him of the darkness he seemed to carry inside, but it hadn't. She felt in her spirit that Beau was trying to fill a void in his life, a void that was consuming him like a vacuum. She didn't have much experience with hearing the Holy Spirit, but somehow, she knew God was trying to tell her that Jesus was the only way to fill the black hole in Beau's life. Even though she knew this episode of Beau's behavior would be over shortly, she began to wonder, could she commit her entire life to a man who didn't know Jesus? Could she become one flesh with a double-minded man?

"I'll talk to him," Eli said. The look he gave Julia spoke volumes. She knew he would honor her relationship with Beau and go to bat for her concerning Beau's hurtful behavior, but she could tell he was torn. She could see the anguish in his face. He genuinely cared for her, and for the first time, she let herself appreciate it. He moved away from her and started toward Beau. Andy and Antonne were already talking to him.

"Bro," Antonne said, "I think it's time for a break." He looked at Heavy and then at Nick. He didn't need to say anything. They could tell he was serious. But instead of taking him seriously, they chose to mock him.

"Aw, thanks dad," Nick said. Heavy followed suit, but instead, he used a nasally high-pitched voice to repeat what Antonne had said.

"What are we, twelve?" Antonne asked sarcastically. "Andy, did you hear that? These fools are still in the seventh grade." Nick stood to his feet abruptly, and Antonne took one step toward him. Antonne was much taller and a little older. What he lacked in physical intimidation, he made up for with Army attitude.

"Alright, alright. Let it be. Not worth getting upset over," Andy said, his voice as calm and soothing as ever.

"Yeah, girls. Don't fight. You're both so pretty." Heavy just couldn't keep from making a joke. Eli hid a smirk. Despite the mounting tension in the room, it was funny.

"Really, Hangdog. I think it's time to go," Andy added.

"I'm not ready to go!" Beau responded.

"Are you listening to me, Marine? I said, I think it's time to go." Andy bent down and spoke firmly. At first, Beau looked like he was going to resist. But then he stood up as best he could and leaned forward, draping an arm around Andy's shoulders.

"This guy saved my life!" he shouted out. His words were slurred and sloppy, but at least, he was on his feet. With his other arm, Beau grabbed Julia and pulled her close. His action was abrupt and possessive, and though she let it happen, she was clearly uncomfortable. "And this beautiful girl right here," Beau's voice was loud enough for the entire bar to hear him, "well, I don't really need to spell it out, but I can tell you she knows where babies come from!" Both of the girls sitting nearby felt their mouths fall open. There was an audible gasp from their table as they looked at each other in shock. No one could believe he had said that.

Julia was so hurt and embarrassed. It was true, she was the mother of his child, but the way he spoke about her in that moment made Julia feel cheap. She felt her face flush with heat. She pulled away from Beau and whispered, "You're embarrassing me. Why would you do that?"

Eli was furious. He could hardly control himself. He could see the tears welling up in Julia's eyes as all the people in the room were looking in their direction. He took one step toward Beau. "You need to go home," he said.

"Who says I need to go home, Eliza?" Beau threw the nickname out, knowing it would irritate his brother.

"I do," he said. He gestured to Andy, Antonne, and Julia, "We do."

"Oh, you mean you perfect people. You sanctimonious, better-than-me people think it's time for me to go home." Beau's words were insulting and hurtful, and it was difficult to remember the fact that he genuinely needed help. Eli was about to snap.

"Watch your mouth, Beau!" Eli shouted. "Before you say something you'll regret."

Beau lunged at Eli, but Eli quickly stepped to the side and Beau fell into one of the high-top tables. When the chair toppled over and crashed to the ground, Nick saw one of the bouncers heading their way. He stood up and walked away from the group, distancing himself. Several of the other guys did the same.

"Is there a problem?" the bouncer asked.

"No, sir. We were just leaving. Right Beau?" Andy replied.

"Yeah, yeah, yeah," Beau said as he staggered past the bouncer, shoving him as he went by. The bouncer said nothing but watched Beau very closely as he made his way to the front door. Eli, Julia, Antonne, and Andy followed close behind. A few members of their group followed them into the parking lot. Julia couldn't tell if they were concerned or entertained.

"I'm driving!" Beau shouted. "Give me the keys!" He could barely stand up, but he was adamant that he would be the one driving them home. Julia held her purse by her side. Since they were riding in her car, she'd been in control of the keys.

"How about I drive," she said, as she walked closer to where he was standing. Without warning, Beau snatched the purse off her arm and held it above his head while he rifled for the keys. Some of Julia's things were falling out onto the asphalt all around them, and as she helplessly crouched to begin picking up her things, she started to cry.

"I said I'm driving!" Beau shouted. "Now get in the car!"

"I ain't gettin' in the car with you!" Antonne shouted back. "You're drunk, a…" he cut himself off and corrected his words. "You're gonna get us all killed!"

"Give me the keys!" Eli said forcefully.

"I'm not getting into that car unless somebody else is driving, Hangdog," Andy added.

"Fine!" Beau screamed. "Julia, get in the car." Julia hesitated as she picked up her remaining few items from the ground. She stood motionless for just a moment, uncertain what to do, and Beau grew impatient. "I said get in the car!" Beau was screaming at the top of his lungs. His nostrils flared and the veins in his neck and face bulged. Julia was frightened. None of them had ever seen him in such a rage. Julia began moving slowly toward the car. She looked back at Andy, Antonne, and Eli as she took a few slow steps toward the passenger side of her vehicle.

"No!" Eli shouted.

"It's okay," Julia tried to sound both reassuring and confident, but she was clearly afraid.

"The car!" Beau screamed again as he pointed toward the waiting vehicle.

Both Andy and Antonne started to say something, but before they could speak, Eli was in Beau's face. "Who do you think you are?" he yelled. "Don't talk to her like that! Don't you ever talk to her that way! She is absolutely amazing and you don't deserve her! You never did!" Eli blurted out before he could stop himself.

Beau stumbled and then pushed Eli backward. He lacked the balance to do much damage, but his situation certainly hadn't dulled his gift for profanity. He hurled expletives at Eli like it was the easiest thing in the world. Antonne turned and looked back toward the door. Several of the group had gone back inside, but a few stood watching in disbelief.

After Beau finished with his string of profane insults, he told the group, "I'm outta here." He then looked at Julia and spread his arms wide. "You're either with me, or you're not? Are you getting in the car, or what?"

Julia began to move toward the car again. The entire situation felt surreal. She wasn't sure how to respond. But, she somehow felt obligated to go with Beau. Eli ran to her as Andy tried in vain to talk sense into Beau. Eli reached for Julia's hand and intentionally laced his fingers between hers. He moved as close to her as he could, so he wouldn't be overheard. "Please, please don't get into that car. Please don't. I'm begging you. If you won't stay for me, stay for Gabe. Please." Julia could hear the sincerity and worry in Eli's voice. She could feel his concern and caring. She glanced up at Andy, who had stepped away from Beau, admitting defeat. She looked back at Eli, whose eyes were glistening with tears as he pleaded with her to stay out of the car. She looked over at Beau and then back at Eli.

"Okay. I'm staying." Her words were soft and hesitant. Eli visibly relaxed, still holding her hand as he led her back to the place where Antonne and Andy were standing.

Julia's choice to stay behind pushed Beau's anger over the edge. He was furious. He screamed, but nobody could understand his words. Then he stumbled toward the car, and Eli let go of Julia's hand to chase him. "Don't go like this! Please, Beau! Don't go!" he called after his brother, who ignored him as he fumbled with the keys.

Beau hung his head out the window and looked back toward Julia. "Last chance!" he called out. Julia shook her head weakly and stepped meekly behind Andy. Beau gritted his teeth and gripped the steering wheel as he started the engine. Their other friends stood silent, nobody said a word. As Beau began to back out, Eli moved over to where Julia stood and grabbed her hand again. He squeezed her fingers between his. He wasn't sure how to feel, or what he should do. He was torn, and so was she.

"You think we should call the police?" Antonne asked. "He outta his mind!"

"As much as I hate to say it, probably," Andy answered.

"He'll never forgive us!" Julia said. "It could ruin his career!"

"Who cares about that right now?" Eli responded. "Better discharged than dead." The group had no choice but to stand back and watch. They stood, huddled together, as Beau backed out in a single jerking movement and made a reckless two-point turn at a dangerously high rate of speed. When Eli saw that the driver's side window was down, he yelled out again, "Beau, stop! Don't! Don't go! I'm calling the cops!" Beau didn't even slow down. Eli couldn't tell if he'd even heard the words. Beau made an erratic turn toward the exit to the parking lot, squalling the tires as he went. Andy pulled out his phone and sighed, disheartened, ready to call the police on his best friend, as he silently prayed for wisdom. Eli ran through the parking lot behind the car as fast as he could, pleading with his twin to stop. Antonne put an arm around Julia, who couldn't stop crying.

No sooner than Andy put his phone to his ear, they all watched in helpless horror as Beau peeled out of the parking lot — right into the path of a large, oncoming utility truck. Antonne cried out powerlessly. The sound of the crash was deafening. It echoed off the walls of the surrounding buildings and was followed instantly by the shriek of squealing tires as the utility driver struggled to bring his truck to a stop. Eli stopped midstride, frozen in his tracks. He could hear nothing but a dull roar inside his head as the shock of the moment ricocheted off every bone in his body. It took him a moment to register the sound of Julia's screams in the background.

The impact of the collision had pushed Julia's tiny car at least twenty yards down the road, maybe more. Andy was already speaking with 9-1-1 dispatch as the group raced, sprinting toward the small, mangled car. The passenger side of the vehicle was completely compressed — crushed all the way in to the center console. The passenger seat was unrecognizable.

The large utility truck was mangled, but, with the exception of some minor scrapes, the driver appeared unhurt. He jumped from the cab of the truck and raced toward the driver's side of Julia's car, where Eli and Antonne were trying to convince a belligerent Beau that he should get out of the car. Beau wouldn't budge. It seemed as though he hadn't even realized what had just happened.

"Are you hurt?" Eli pleaded with Beau for an answer. He could see a red stripe across Beau's neck where the seatbelt had nearly broken the skin. "You have to get out Beau. If you're not hurt, you have to get out."

The driver of the truck began to grow frantic as he noted the smoke rolling out from under the hood of Julia's car. "He needs to get out. It might catch fire. Get out, kid. Now!"

"Please, Beau." Julia was sobbing at the window, begging Beau to be reasonable, but Beau was still in a rage and seemed ready to pass out.

"That's it!" Eli yelled as he yanked up on the handle of the driver's door. Nothing. He checked to see if the door was locked, but it wasn't. "It's stuck." He turned to Andy. "Andy, do you have your knife?" Andy reached into his pocket and pulled out the pocket knife he always carried. He quickly tossed it to Eli and stepped closer, even as he held the phone to his ear.

"They're on their way," he told the others.

"I might need your help Antonne." Eli looked in Antonne's direction as he took charge. He reached into the car through the window and, though Beau was clawing and pawing at him, he managed to cut the seatbelt with Andy's knife. He didn't pause to consider the irony that, despite all that had happened, Beau had still managed to put on his seatbelt. Eli was trying to determine how he'd pull Beau through the driver's side window as the smell of smoke grew stronger. Just then, the driver of the utility truck hastily returned to the car with the crowbar he carried in the cab of his truck.

"Let's try this!" He jammed the crowbar into the crack where the door met the body of the car and began to pry. "Pull!" Antonne and Eli each reached into the car and gripped the window opening and began to pull.

Andy handed his phone to Julia without a word and moved toward the car. As low flames began to flicker under the hood, the driver grew more panicked. "Pull! Pull!" The driver screamed as a few other onlookers rushed over to see if there was a way to help. "I might have an extinguisher," the driver told them. "Go look!" Two men rushed toward the utility truck, frantically searching for a way to extinguish the growing flame.

There was no room for Andy to squeeze in next to Antonne, so he did the only thing he knew how to do. He placed his hand on the back of the car and began to call out to God. He loudly and boldly asked God to send a band of angels to loose the door. Julia reached out and took his hand, joining him in his prayer. Almost as soon as his words hit the air, the driver's side door flew open and Antonne, Eli, and the truck driver all fell backward onto the asphalt behind them. Beau slumped sideways and helplessly slid awkwardly out of the seat and onto the ground. His legs were still inside the car when the truck driver grabbed him under his arms and pulled him onto the parking lot asphalt. Beau slurred and yelled and batted the air like he was trying to fight, but to no avail. Instead, he looked pitiful, almost pathetic, as the group looked on.

Eli rubbed his face with his hands as the two Samaritans did their best to extinguish the growing flames under the hood of Julia's car. As the flames spread, the entire group sat panting, in both disbelief and shock. Tears flowed down Julia's cheeks as the sound of sirens grew closer and closer. Her heart broke for Beau, but also for herself. Eli moved closer to where she sat and whispered, "I'm so glad you didn't get in that car." Julia closed her eyes as she realized how close she'd come to death, and she couldn't help but be grateful for Eli. Even though she couldn't return it, his love for her had saved her life, and they both knew it.

HANGDOG III

The Absolution

PART TWO

CHAPTER THIRTEEN

Beau didn't argue as the police officer placed the cuffs on his wrists. He was still wobbly and slurring his speech, but the fight seemed to have finally left him. Eli and Andy, Julia and Antonne sat watching on the curb near the squad car, having answered all the questions the officers asked, including questions about drug use. Andy turned and looked toward the door of the bar. The group of eager onlookers had disappeared, thankfully. Eli stood up and approached one of policemen. He was young and fit and seemed like he might be easy to talk to. "Excuse me, sir?" Eli asked.

"Yeah?" the officer answered quickly and then immediately responded to the voice coming through his radio.

Eli waited till he was finished talking and then asked, "What will happen now? What should we do?" Eli felt helpless, sort of like a lost child. Because the officer could sense Eli's earnestness, he turned his full attention to him and carefully spelled out the next steps. The officer told Eli that Beau had been arrested for DWI and he mentioned bail and arraignment and told Eli where to go to start the ball rolling. Since the EMTs found nothing immediately wrong with Beau, apart from his inebriation, he'd go to jail immediately. Eli thanked the officer and turned toward his friends. He walked slowly, his head hanging down as he watched his own shoes move across the asphalt. His anger was gone and now all he could feel was sorrow. He couldn't believe how this night of celebration had gone so wrong. He silently sat back on the curb and stared at the crushed side of Julia's car. The lights from the wrecker bounced harshly off the crumpled metal, and Eli closed his eyes to thank God it hadn't been worse.

After a few moments, Antonne broke the silence with a question none of them wanted to ask, "Who's gonna call Mr. Joe and Ms. Val? One of us has to."

"Not it," Andy said, without a trace of humor in his voice.

"I'll do it," Eli announced. *It should be me.* He stood up and reached into his back pocket for his phone.

"Wait," Andy said, his voice pensive. He was obviously being careful with his words. "I think we need to talk this through."

"What do you mean? Talk what through?" Eli asked. He'd been doing his best to remain calm, but he was on edge and he sorely longed for peace that surpassed understanding. For some reason, the amplified sense of peace he'd felt since waking from his coma had been evaporating in the past several weeks.

"Well, we need to decide what to tell your parents, and how to say it. Are you going to tell them *everything*, or just keep it to tonight's events?" Andy looked around the group questioningly. In his spirit, he knew the truth would set Beau free — but was it their place to tell that truth, or was it his?

"You mean, am I going to tell them Beau's a drug addict and a drunk?" Eli spoke callously, without thinking. His words tore through the air like a hot dagger, and he regretted them immediately.

"What?" Julia asked, shock and disbelief in her voice. "What do you mean a drug addict?"

Eli let out a deep sigh and let his head fall backward until he was staring at the night sky. He put his hand to his eyes and rubbed his face, frustrated with the situation and with himself. "I… well… maybe I shouldn't be the one to say it, but somebody has to." Eli looked up and made eye contact first with Andy and then with Antonne. "She needs to know, right?"

Antonne looked at Andy and then back at Eli. He nodded. "She does," he agreed.

Andy was silent. She did need to know, for her sake and for the sake of their son, but this definitely wasn't the ideal situation for breaking such heavy news. He looked back at Eli and nodded once slowly.

"Look, Julia, I know you've noticed Beau's weird behavior, how he sleeps so much now and seems up one minute and then down the next. I've heard you mention it. Well, you should know that it's not just because he's stressed out over his med review. It's because he's addicted to pain pills. He's taking them all the time. I think he mixed them with booze tonight and that's how we ended up in this situation!" Eli was both hurt and angered by Beau's behavior. He spoke harshly, "Let's just get it all out there, okay? On the night Gabe was born..."

"Eli, wait," Andy spoke up. "Tread lightly here, okay?" He gave Eli a knowing look. Antonne was in the dark about what happened on that night, but nodded at Andy's suggestion anyway.

Eli took a deep breath and softened his tone. He walked over and sat next to Julia. "On the night Gabe was born, we were late because Beau was passed out. We think he'd had too many of his pills and that he'd been drinking, and I don't know what all else he might have taken, but we had to drag him to Andy's truck…"

Julia was fighting tears. "Stop," she said softly. "I think I already knew it. I don't know how I knew, I just knew. He hasn't been the same." She hung her head, saddened. "I didn't want to believe it, but something in me has known it all along. He hasn't exactly been a master at hiding it." She smiled slightly through her tears and wiped her eyes. The group sat silently for a minute before she spoke again, "Now what do we do?"

"We call mom and dad and then we go from there I guess." Eli looked at his phone again and pulled up Valerie's number. The photo of her smiling back at him caused tears to fill his eyes. Because he was so angry with Beau, he thought telling his parents would be the easiest thing in the world, but now that he faced the actual task, telling them felt like the hardest thing in the world. He knew this would break their hearts.

Antonne moved closer to Julia and put one of his long arms around her as her tears fell quietly. This kind gesture was more than her frayed emotions could bear. She was both hurting and grateful to be alive at the same time, and she found herself weeping freely in Antonne's arms as he watched Eli pacing the same ten feet over and over in front of them.

Andy was quiet. He'd been praying and praying that Beau would get help and that God would turn everything around for him and that he'd be forced to face the truth and step into the light. And though he recognized the night's events as an answer to prayer — this definitely wasn't what he had in mind.

Eli held his breath as he waited for his mom to pick up. He knew calling so late at night would jolt her awake instantly. Nobody ever calls someone in the middle of the night unless something bad has happened. He heard the sleep and urgency in her voice when she answered, and he also heard fear. The others looked on as Eli opened his mouth, forcing the words out, "Mom? I… I have something to tell you…"

CHAPTER FOURTEEN

Valerie sat with one hand on Beau's back and the other tightly gripping Joe's fingers as they waited for the administrator to return. Julia gently rocked Gabe in his carrier as he napped. For a brief moment, she marveled at how much he'd grown. He'd soon be walking, and time seemed to be passing both quickly and slowly at the same time. She sat over from Beau and watched the side of his face intently. He was so very, very broken. His eyes were sunken, and he looked really tired. His baseball cap was pulled low on his brow, and his hair was longer than it had been in years. The room was eerily quiet. The only sounds were those of air pushing through the vents and the faint clicking of a tabletop clock on the mahogany desk at the front of the room.

Julia took a deep breath and let it out slowly. Valerie turned toward her and smiled slightly. She nodded as if to ask, "Are you okay?" and Julia nodded in return. Without realizing it, they both then turned their focus toward the search for silver linings. They both sat in silence, each unbeknownst to the other, thanking God for the few blessings they could see through the dense spiritual fog that had surrounded them all for months. Things could have been so much worse, but most days, it didn't feel like it.

The months leading up to this day had been some of the hardest they'd ever experienced as a family. Everything seemed dark. If not for a few bright spots that perforated the blackness and the peace she could attribute only to the Holy Spirit, Julia may have truly considered taking Gabe and walking away from it all. Thankfully though, the bright spots, her love for Beau, and her efforts to draw near to God kept her both sane and stable. As she mulled over the truth of their current reality, the door to the office opened. A tall, slim, gray haired man with a neat beard and a kindly expression entered the room. He almost glided as he walked and he smiled a genuine smile as he moved toward the desk in the front of the room. His button-down shirt was tucked neatly into a pair of gray slacks and his thin, black belt appeared to match his loafers perfectly. He looked put together, but not pretentious. He gave his mouth a quick swipe with a paper napkin. "Sorry about the wait! I have been running behind all day! My name is Robert Taft. I'm the patient coordinator and also a counselor here. You must be Beau." Taft held his hand out to Beau. And although Beau shook his hand, he kept his eyes cast downward toward the floor. Taft smiled slightly, as if he knew how Beau was feeling. Beau had been wearing his shame like an albatross around his neck since the moment his parents posted his bail. He hadn't been able to look his father in the eye for months, he'd barely spoken to Eli, and when the reality of his addiction came fully into the light, just getting out of bed had become an insurmountable task. Up until recently, he thought he could beat it with willpower alone. He honestly believed he could simply walk away. But he'd failed.

In the midst of his legal proceedings, Beau's reputation as an outstanding Marine prior to his convoy attack had earned him the respect, and ultimately the kindness, of his commanding officer. He would not face a court martial and would instead be allowed a quiet, honorable discharge at the end of his current enlistment as a result of his pending medical evaluation. As a requirement, Beau had been required to attend an outpatient substance abuse program that lasted two months. Despite the kindness of the Corps, and Beau's successful completion of the substance abuse program, losing what he believed to be his identity as a Marine had all but crushed his spirit and, though he'd cut back, he continued using. He fell back into the dark pit of addiction less than a week after he completed the program.

On top of that, Joe had been able to, once again, secure JP Sapuro as Beau's attorney. Thanks to JP's efforts, a separate outpatient drug and alcohol counseling program had been made mandatory by the judge presiding over Beau's case. In exchange for the successful completion of the program, the charges of felonious reckless endangerment and intoxication assault would be dropped, leaving only the DUI on his record. This time, Beau had seemed dedicated and determined. He had suffered through days of detox at home in order to adhere to the program's expectations. He completed the steps and passed every single drug test the counselors had administered for ten whole weeks. But the very day after graduation, he learned that one of the Marines he had served with in Afghanistan, a Marine who was part of his convoy on the day of the attack, had committed suicide. After sitting alone in his bedroom for an hour, Beau pulled the oxycodone pills from under his nightstand where they were hidden, and then he stole Eli's truck and drove into the night. They finally found him at bar downtown, passed out in a corner booth.

That same night, Joe called a family meeting while Beau slept it off upstairs. He told everyone that the time had come for desperate measures, and with the support of Valerie, Eli, Julia, Antonne and even Andy, live from Afghanistan via Skype, he had come to the decision to make inpatient rehab a requirement for Beau, particularly if he wanted to continue living under their roof with Julia and Gabe. As it stood, Julia almost never left Gabe alone with Beau, just in case. Even Beau knew she didn't trust him with Gabe's care completely, and it had become a sticking point in their relationship. But when all was said and done, the family had been able to convince a tearful, broken Beau that an inpatient facility was exactly what he needed for long-term recovery. Nobody *wanted* it — nobody had wanted any of it, but they'd already exhausted all their other options, they'd already tried everything else they could think of.

"It's nice to meet you, son," Taft said as he looked at Beau. He then turned his attention to the entire group. "As you know, this is a Christian, inpatient treatment facility. We will do our very best to encourage both practical and spiritual healing during Beau's stay. However, for the first few weeks, there will be no contact with family. You all and," Mr. Taft paused as he looked down at the stack of papers in front of him, "it says here there are also two brothers in the home? Eli and Antonio?"

Joe and Valerie exchanged a glance. "It's Antonne," Valerie began, "but he's…" Joe stopped her with a glance as he placed a hand on her knee. For all intents and purposes, Antonne *was* part of the family, and Joe saw no reason to try to explain.

"Oh, I'm sorry, Antonne." He cleared his throat. "You will all attend family therapy sessions once per week." Valerie nodded her understanding before Joe spoke up.

"Will I need to plan to miss work for the sessions?"

"We will do our best to work with your schedules. In some cases, it may be necessary to take a couple hours off. Typically, the sessions last one hour, but we find that most families enjoy some time together afterward." Taft smiled again. He seemed genuinely kind and loving. Julia liked him immediately. Mr. Taft began to explain what Beau could expect during his stay. He spoke of a medically supervised detox period, private counseling sessions, groups sessions, exercise, even skills classes like cooking and personal finance.

As the meeting continued inside, Eli sat alone in his truck in the parking lot. After arriving at the rehab facility, he had been unable to go inside. He physically couldn't make himself get out of the truck. He texted his parents <I DON'T THINK I CAN DO THIS> and simply stayed put. He knew this was where Beau needed to be for himself and for their family, but he also knew that his relationship with Beau may never be the same again and facing him in that environment felt impossible. After all, it was Eli who'd told his parents about Beau's addiction. And on the night of the accident, in a flurry of anger and pain, he'd also told Julia all of Beau's secrets, including where he'd been the night Gabe was born. And then, perhaps worst of all, one night, after arriving home from a young people's Bible study they'd attended together, Eli confessed to Julia that he believed God had given him feelings for her in order to spare her life on the night of the accident. If he hadn't been so in love with her, and so adamant and sincere in his pleas, she likely would have gotten into the car with Beau. Given the state of the vehicle after the crash, the likelihood of surviving the accident would have been slim to none. As Eli explained how he believed the Holy Spirit had ordained his feelings for her in order to save her life and then continued on to tell Julia that he still cared for her, but that his intense, romantic feelings had faded dramatically after that night, Beau had been standing outside the door, listening to every word. He'd come around the corner with both pain and anger in his expression. He had immediately assumed the two were engaged in a relationship behind his back. It had taken weeks for Julia to convince Beau that nothing had happened between her and Eli. It had taken even longer than that for Eli to convince Beau that his feelings for Julia were gone. He loved her, but like a sister. He couldn't explain how the feelings started or why they stopped, but he felt strongly that it was by God's design. Despite all the talking and pleading and explaining, jealousy and mistrust had become a part of their daily lives. As Beau continued to wrestle with his own spirituality, these feelings of mistrust toward his brother had become a good excuse for shutting God out. Now, Eli couldn't even enter a room with Julia without being interrogated. The only reprieve he got was when he cared for Gabe. There was a bond between Eli and Gabe that even Beau could see. Eli loved Gabe dearly.

All in all, the entire family was exhausted. Everyone had struggled and was continuing to struggle. Each day was a battle.

Eli hung his head. He was afraid to go in, afraid that he might have to confront his own anger toward Beau and his decisions. He was afraid that he might have to confess some of the darkness, anger and envy in his own heart. Darkness he didn't even know he had until being confronted with Beau's addiction. He longed to feel the peace and contentment he'd felt in those months following his coma. Somehow, God had been so tangible in his life during that time. Losing Ivy and, in a way, losing Beau had somehow caused him to take his eyes off of God's goodness. As tears filled his eyes, he asked God for wisdom. He asked God for forgiveness and for the return of the peace he'd been missing for months.

Eli felt as though his heart had been torn open. He allowed his mind to drift back through time as he thought about the course of action that had brought them to this day. He thought about graduation, about the accident, about losing two years of living to a coma, about losing Ivy, about Beau's injuries in the convoy attack, about becoming an uncle, about watching Beau's spiral into addiction and about the strange place of limbo he'd been living in since being released from physical therapy. "I'm closing in on twenty-two and I am stuck. I don't know what to do with my life. I don't know what to do for my brother. I don't know what to do." He called out to God, "What should I do? What do *You* want me to do God?"

And at that exact moment, it suddenly hit Eli like a ton of bricks — that was the first time he'd asked God for direction in months and months and it was the first time he'd felt the true power of prayer since Andy had headed back to North Carolina. He felt a pang of conviction before silently thanking God in advance for His provision and His promises. Eli wanted to pray like Andy. He wanted to see God the way Andy saw God. Eli was sitting in silence, waiting on God to speak to him when he felt the overwhelming urge to go inside the office to be with his family. He knew immediately it was God. But he recoiled at the thought. He didn't want to go in, but God's voice in his heart was crystal clear — perhaps more so than it had ever been — so he opened the door to his truck and stepped out. He locked the doors behind him, placed his keys into his pocket and made his way to the front doors of the building.

A receptionist with short brown hair and petite features greeted him. Eli told her he was late for a meeting and was quickly directed to the office on the opposite side of the room. The wall was made of windows, but the windows were obscured by white plantation blinds. Even the door was covered by blinds. The only thing Eli could see through the slats as he neared the door was Beau's left leg, bouncing up and down anxiously. He turned the knob on the door and pushed it open. "I'm sorry to interrupt," he said. "I almost decided not to come in." He was being bluntly honest, but he delivered his words in a way that Mr. Taft found endearing.

Taft did a double take when he noticed that Beau and Eli were twins. He chuckled, "I can't say it's the first time I've heard something like that." He stood and reached a hand out toward Eli, "And you are?"

"Eli."

"Eli. I thought so, but didn't want to assume. Please take a seat. We'll be wrapping up with the verbal orientation soon. We'll get all the paperwork out of the way, then I'll take you all on a quick tour." He turned to Beau, "During our tour, an orderly will take your belongings for inspection and deliver them to your room. Once you've said goodbye to your family, I'll personally walk you up and help you get settled.

Just thinking about their goodbyes made Julia's heart ache. Valerie was still gripping Joe's fingers and patting Beau's back. The action likely brought her more comfort than it brought Beau. Eli moved to a row of three chairs near the seat his father had chosen. Joe shot Eli an understanding look. Eli hadn't meant to tune out the rest of the discussion, but his mind was preoccupied with the idea of yet another goodbye. It seemed like he'd endured too many goodbyes already. He desperately wanted Beau to know that he loved him, no matter what they'd been through. But, he knew Beau didn't want to hear anything he had to say at the moment. He also knew he probably couldn't even bring himself to speak the words aloud anyway. As he sat there thinking about everything he and his brother had faced, he knew he needed a way to tell Beau how he felt *without* words — a way that reached beyond words. He leaned forward and rested his elbows on his knees, looking down at the patterned carpet beneath his feet. As Mr. Taft's voice continued to fill the air with a muffled melody, he noticed the contrast between his bright, white socks and the maroon rug that lined the office floor. He was instantly reminded of all the times Beau had joking left dirty socks on his pillow while they were growing up. What started as a brotherly annoyance had become Beau's signature move. Eli smiled at that memory and then almost choked on a sob forming in his throat. He wanted his brother back. And then, it hit him — Eli knew instantly what he had to do to tell Beau how much he cared. He began plotting immediately. As soon as he had the chance, he would excuse himself to the restroom in the lobby. He'd take off his shoes and his socks and put his socks in his pockets. When the time finally came to say goodbye, he'd hug his brother and quietly leave those socks behind, right on Beau's shoulders.

CHAPTER FIFTEEN

The house was strangely quiet as Joe and Valerie, Eli, Antonne, Julia and baby Gabe gathered around the television for a typical family movie night. It had been several months since they last spent time together at home. It felt strange not having Beau around, but the reports from the rehab center had been positive so far. The family counseling sessions had shed light on lots of things that none of them really wanted to talk about. For example, Eli had no intention of sharing with his family how truly angry he was with Beau — even though everyone already knew. Julia had shared about her fears of the future, in her worry about the possibility of raising Gabe without a father or with an addict. All of the variables and the unknowns had come rising up out of her and it had felt good to have it all out in the open. Valerie and Joe felt more solidified in their relationship than they had in years, and though they had always had what they thought of as the perfect relationship, they felt a strange sense of renewal and hopefulness for the future.

Valerie decided to make an extra batch of popcorn before the movie started. As she trotted off to the kitchen, everyone settled in to a comfortable position while Gabe played on the rug. Eli sat on the floor next to the baby, tickling him and allowing Gabe to climb all over his lap. He found himself laughing simply because Gabe laughed and the sound of a baby's laughter is always infectious. Julia held out a freshly made bottle and spoke to Gabe as if he were a little man, "Gabey, do you want your bottle?"

Gabe immediately crawled across the floor to his mother as Joe watched. "If only they stayed that responsive and agreeable," he chuckled. Julia giggled as Gabe wrapped both his chubby hands around the bottle and rolled over onto his back. Antonne took the opportunity to open a discussion with Joe about work. Antonne had proven to be an outstanding employee and, though everyone at his work seemed to love him, he couldn't shake the feeling that he was meant to be somewhere else.

Eli listened, and the words "somewhere else" echoed inside his head. He laid his head back against the ottoman and stared at the ceiling. Somehow, he still felt so unsettled. His life was not at all what he had expected it to be. And though he was back at school working through his core curriculum, he still had no idea what he wanted to major in and no idea what he wanted to be. He closed his eyes and silently asked God for direction, "I want my joy back, Lord. What do you want me to do? Who am I supposed to be? Why am I in this situation? Please speak to me. Tell me, show me what you want me to do. Forgive me for being so hard-headed. I just need peace." Eli was startled when he heard a response from God almost immediately. It was as if his mind became flooded with promise after promise found in Scripture. He had a vision of the pages of Scripture being turned rapidly, but he could still read the text, and the text that he saw was one promise of God after another. It dawned on Eli that it wasn't God who had changed, and God certainly hadn't pushed him aside.

The very second that Eli realized that God's love, peace, and provision was his for the taking, he was overcome by an inspiring sense of calm. When he thought about the fact that he did not have to *do* anything to earn God's love, and that he could rely on every promise of God all the time, he realized that he had nothing to be upset about. Sure, there were still problems, and sure, the family was still facing some tall odds. And no, he didn't immediately know what God wanted him to do with his life, but he knew for a fact that everything was going to be okay and the answer would come as long as he kept God in first place. He closed his eyes and soaked in the joy of that moment. He made it a point to focus on the blessings in his life. He laughed at himself and he could almost hear Andy's voice saying "I told you so."

Finally, Valerie came back and the smell of freshly made popcorn filled the air. She handed out bowls to everyone and passed around the large bag of popcorn so each person could get what they wanted. Joe grabbed the remote and Julia turned off the lamp that rested on the end table by the sofa. Gabe was almost asleep and Antonne had somehow managed to fold both his long, gangly legs in front of him on the love seat — without complaining of knee pain. Antonne had walked with a perpetual limp, which he called his "strut," since the Army released him, and certain movements always caused him pain, so his current posture was a momentous achievement.

About thirty minutes into the movie, Eli began to feel groggy. And though he tried to fight it, when he rested his head back on the ottoman, he fell asleep. While his family continued to watch the movie, he rested, undisturbed. Valerie smiled at the sight of him. She so enjoyed moments like these. Val touched Joe's hand and nodded toward Eli. Joe looked at his son, dozing with his head back and mouth slightly open, and smiled back at Val. But, neither of them could have guessed what was going on inside his head.

As Eli slept, he found himself transported to a different place. It felt familiar, like he had been there before. He knew he was dreaming, but he knew it was more than a dream at the same time. He walked through a field of green grass, between rows of the most beautiful wildflowers he'd ever seen — unique, vivid, like nothing he'd seen on earth — blowing lightly in the breeze. The air was clean and fragrant and beautifully sweet, it was neither cold nor warm.

Eli knew, somehow, that he needed to keep walking until he reached the top of a low, rolling hill that lay ahead of him. This thought startled him. How did he know that? He kept walking. He wanted to run. Something about this place felt right. He was elated and strangely peaceful at the same time. He looked around and took in an array of vivid, beautiful colors, unlike any he'd seen before. He noticed the melodic sounds of a stream trickling somewhere nearby.

When he finally reached the top of the hill, about twenty yards ahead of him, he could see the back of a man with dark hair wearing a long, elaborate robe. The man radiated with a brilliant light. Eli knew, somehow, that this man was Jesus, and yet being there with him felt as natural as breathing. Eli walked toward the man. As he got within just a few feet, the man reached out his right arm, as if beckoning Eli to stand with him. Eli wasn't afraid, he was comforted. It almost felt like returning home after a long trip. Eli continued to move closer to him, until his arm came down on Eli's shoulder. Eli could feel the weight of it against his back. He wanted to turn and look at this man — this man he somehow knew to be Christ — but he couldn't. He physically couldn't turn away. Instead, something held him transfixed in the distance. He looked straight ahead, staring at the horizon. There before him, in a shallow valley, bathed in rose gold light that reminded Eli of a sunset, was a city unlike anything he had ever seen. It felt like only seconds had passed when a soft, pale orange mist that seemed to radiate light all by itself began to roll in around them. The mist rose until it obscured Eli's view of what he instinctively knew to be Heaven's gates. It all felt so familiar. Eli had visited this place before — he knew it. Finally, with the mist rolling in, Eli broke his gaze away from the city, letting his eyes fall to his own feet. "I'm barefoot," he thought, and slowly turned his face toward Jesus. He heard a laugh, and then lifted his eyes until he was face to face with the Messiah. The light that was radiating from Him seemed to be alive, and Eli almost shielded his eyes.

Eli's immediate instinct was to fall on his knees. Through the light, he saw kind eyes and a wide smile set above a dark beard. He sat on his knees, frozen in time, washed in a feeling of pure love like nothing he'd ever experienced. He knelt, full of joy, on the verge of weeping, speechless, and unable to move. Eli finally mustered the ability to open his mouth, but he never got the chance. Jesus lifted his right hand and laid it on Eli's head, right where a piece of his skull had been removed after the accident. Instantly, Eli remembered. He had been here before!

Then, without warning, it was as though all of Eli's questions about his life were answered. He suddenly knew his path. He understood his mission. He knew what he was supposed to do. And he also knew it was time to wake up.

CHAPTER SIXTEEN

Beau sat quietly on his tiny bed, staring out the window into the courtyard. The week before had been one of the longest weeks of his life, second only to the week following the accident — when he learned that he was the cause of the accident and the reason Eli had slipped into a coma and might not survive. For the first time in what seemed like forever, he woke up without pain radiating throughout his body. He woke up without feeling like everything around him was gray and foggy. He didn't feel angry, agitated, sad, or anxious. For the first time in a long time, he felt *normal*.

He took a deep breath, filling his lungs with the cool air in the room, and thought about something his counselor had said, "Rehab is like war and fighting through withdrawals is like a battle. You can win the war, but you will never forget the battle — you *should* never forget the battle — because forgetting the battle undermines your victory in the war." He hadn't really thought about his situation in that way. But after spending some time with other veterans who were dealing with similar struggles, viewing his situation as though it were a mission somehow made him more focused on the outcome. He really wasn't the only one struggling.

Without warning, Eli entered Beau's mind. He released his deep breath and turned to look at the shelf above his desk. There, in a little round ball, were Eli socks. A pang of guilt pierced Beau's heart. On the day he had arrived at rehab, when Eli said goodbye and hugged him, leaving behind his socks, Beau knew the message he was trying to convey. But, he had chosen to shut his brother out. He didn't respond, he didn't laugh. He simply took the socks and balled them in his fist. Now that his head was clear, he wanted nothing more than to tell his brother everything was okay. He wanted Eli to know that he wouldn't waste any more time being angry. He also wanted him to know that he felt a strange kind of gratitude. If Eli had never developed feelings for Julia, if he hadn't cared for her enough to beg her to stay behind with him that night at the bar, she likely wouldn't have survived. Beau closed his eyes tightly. When he thought about what might have been, it was like a dagger to his heart. And when he thought about the fact that his brother's short-lived love for Julia likely saved her life, he found himself forced to acknowledge the possibility of supernatural intervention. Could it really be possible that God gave Eli feelings for Julia just long enough to save her life? Could that be real? Being surrounded by so many people of faith at the rehab facility, people he didn't know — people who didn't know his history, his story, or his failures — somehow made it easier for him explore the possibility of faith, a possibility that he had been fighting against for so long. Somehow it felt different coming from strangers than it did from his family. Maybe it had been his pride. Maybe it had been guilt. Whatever the reason, none of it mattered anymore. As he sat there thinking, Beau realized that being in rehab made him feel kind of like he had felt when he joined the Marines. His past was completely unknown. He was free to be whoever he wanted to be. Everyone was just like him — everyone was on even ground. He still wore his shame like a wet blanket, but nobody there knew about it, and he didn't care what his counselors and the psychiatrist expected, he had no plans to come clean.

His mind wandered back to the possibility of God. Could he really deny the wave of miracles in his past? Suddenly, he was back in his convoy — he saw his fellow Marines being pulled from the burning vehicle ahead of him.

He could hear the chaos and the sounds of explosions all around him. He could feel the searing pain shooting through his body. He could smell the dust and hot metal. As his mind reeled, he had trouble catching his breath. His chest tightened. He started to cry out, but then he heard the sound of Andy's voice calling out to God. This time, he felt the peace that had befallen the battle field that day. He could sense the awe that his crew had experienced. He knew — *knew* — it was God. He covered his face with his hands and tried to regain control of his breathing. He physically shook the thoughts from his head by rubbing his fingers over his eyes and hair. "No," he thought. It couldn't be that. He needed to believe that everything he'd endured was punishment for his past transgressions — a kind of karma. He deserved everything he got. If God had really intervened that day, He had done it for Andy, no one else — definitely not for him.

Beau took a few minutes to regain his composure. He stood on shaky legs and walked to the mirror above his small sink. He was surprised to find that his face was wet with sweat. He turned on the faucet and let the cool water run over his hands. For the first time in days, he wanted to use. He craved the numb that came over him when he washed pills down with whiskey. He gripped the sides of the sink and gritted his teeth. He thought he'd already weathered that part of the storm, that he had already fought that battle. It was as if something outside himself was trying to entice him. He could feel heaviness, a repression, unlike anything he'd ever experienced. "No!" this time he shouted. As soon as the word escaped his lips, the heavy feeling dissipated slowly, and Beau realized he really did want to heal — and he hadn't known it for sure until that very moment. He stood up, staring at himself in the mirror. He took a deep breath and blew it out, calming himself. He glanced at the digital clock by his bed. He had a group session.

Everyone working at the facility seemed so open to his questions. When he first arrived, he had put a wall around himself with his typical cynicism, but everyone there seemed completely unfazed by his behavior. No one seemed offended or upset. In fact, it was almost as if no one even noticed. This alone had resulted in Beau letting his guard down, at least some. In a recent meeting with Mr. Taft, he had been confronted with a question that had been on his mind ever since, "If you were the only person on earth and nothing had ever created bias in you — no religion, no science, no cultural influences — and it was your job to look at the majesty of planet Earth and make a decision: God's creation or happy accident, which would you choose?" Beau thought about his family's trip to the Grand Canyon. He thought about all the times he and his brother watched the sunrise and the sunset over the lake, he thought about his mom's flowers and the huge oak tree in their yard. He thought about the ocean and the clouds and the blueness of the sky. If a painting is proof of a painter and a building is proof of a builder — then why is it considered unreasonable to believe that all of creation is proof of the Creator?

As Beau stood thinking about everything that had happened in his life up to this point, while preparing to sit down with a group of other men who were all struggling, and about just how far he'd actually come in only a week, he felt an unexpected anticipation, an excitement even, for what the rest of his time here might bring. He felt strangely empowered by his desire to get better. He looked down at the floor beneath his feet and scoffed at his own resistance to coming here. He hadn't wanted to come. He had never wanted to be here. But after just a week, he didn't want to leave.

CHAPTER SEVENTEEN

"You're not going to believe what came in the mail yesterday! I meant to tell you last night, but it completely slipped my mind," Valerie said as she placed a tray of biscuits on the breakfast table.

"Well, don't leave us hangin' Mom," Eli responded, as he shoved half a biscuit into his mouth. Julia shook her head as the crumbs spilled all over Eli's shirt. She spooned another bite of peaches into Gabe's mouth and wiped his little chin with a paper towel. He had mastered feeding himself small bites of solid food, but using a spoon was still an inevitable mess.

"Do tell, Babe… I have to get going or I'm going to be late," Joe said. He had an early meeting and was more rushed than usual.

"A wedding invitation from Kevin and Maggie!" Valerie's eyes grew wide in anticipation of her family's response to the news.

"What!" Eli said in disbelief. "Didn't they just get engaged last month?"

"They did," Val nodded, "but word on the street is Kevin got orders to Aviano in Italy and now they're trying to pull off a miracle wedding before it's time for him to be there."

"Wow!" Joe responded. "I can't believe it! Kevin is still an awkward, goofy kid in my mind."

Val laughed, "Mine too!"

"And who are Kevin and Maggie exactly? Are these people I should remember or not?" Antonne finally spoke up. He'd been too busy filling his belly to do much talking.

Eli laughed out loud, "Poor Ant, he never knows half the people we talk about."

"Kevin Hinkley is the youth pastor's son. Maggie went to school with the boys. Kevin did too, but Maggie didn't attend our church at the time. They've been dating since right after high school. And now, they're getting married in just under six weeks!" Valerie made a squealing sound and clapped her hands together rapidly in front of her chest, indicating her immense enthusiasm and love for all things romantic.

"Oh my gosh! Total sidebar, but you just called him Ant! I love it! How long have you been calling him that?" She looked at Eli, but Antonne answered instead.

"A couple weeks probably. At first he did it to annoy me, but it grew on me. So now I don't mind." He popped a strawberry into his mouth and smiled, both cheeks as full as they could be.

"Yeah, it totally sucked the fun out of it for me, too," Eli added, shaking his head.

Joe stood and walked over to Valerie, kissed her tenderly on the forehead and said, "I should be home by dinner. I love you."

"I love you, too!" Val sang. "Be careful!"

Julia loved watching Joe and Val together. It gave her hope to see two people still so in love after so long. She'd missed out on that after her parents divorced, and she never got tired of seeing it.

As Joe walked behind Antonne, he gave him a light tap on the top of his head, "Tell them what we were talking about last night, son. They might know something I don't. Love you all, bye!" Joe grabbed his suit coat and his briefcase and headed out.

"Well?" Eli asked immediately. "What were you two talking about last night?"

Antonne wiped his mouth with his napkin. Valerie walked to the table with her coffee and sat down. "We're all ears!" she said.

Julia placed a few pieces of cereal on Gabe's tray to keep him occupied while she finished her breakfast. He immediately grasped a piece between his chubby fingers and went to work. "Yep," she added.

"Well," Antonne began, "in the last week or so, I've developed this weird desire to learn computers, like systems and programs. But I've always hated computers. I only learned to type because they made me, but now, it's like I can't stop thinking about it. I mean, legit, I think about learning computers as much as I think about girls — and that's pretty much all the time." Everyone laughed and Valerie shook her head with a smile.

"Well, that sounds like the Lord to me, sweet boy," Valerie said. "An honorable desire that comes out of nowhere that is completely opposite from anything you wanted to do before could be a calling! Maybe God's trying to tell you something."

"That's exactly what Mr. Joe said," Antonne answered.

"Well, he *is* a smart man." Val raised her eyebrows, "He married me, didn't he?" She laughed at her own joke. Eli rolled his eyes and made a groaning sound. Julia giggled.

Antonne smiled, "Well played Mrs. V, well played."

"I agree," said Julia. "If it's the desire of your heart, maybe God put it there." She had been studying the Word diligently since the day she accepted Christ as her Savior. Valerie was continually impressed by how much wisdom she had gained in such a short period of time. "I think you owe it to yourself to consider the fact that maybe God is calling you down a path you'd never choose to go on. You know, a 'it had to be God' kind of thing?"

"Maybe so," Antonne added. "Definitely not one I would've picked for myself. But, the idea of not doing it makes me feel like I would regret it. I mean, I really, really want to do it. But I'm also worried that I'll only really want to do it for a little while and then I will have wasted all that money and time. What if I start doing it and hate it? I mean, it's not exactly an exciting choice. What if I get bored?"

"My heart tells me you won't regret it," Valerie answered. "Something about this feels right."

Eli had remained silent. He carefully considered Antonne's experience, and then he decided it was time for him to speak up, too. "You know, it's funny that you suddenly want to do something you never would've thought about doing before and here we are, talking about maybe God calling you into that career. Well, I haven't told you all this, but the other night during the movie, when I dozed off, I know for a fact that God told me that I was supposed to go into business administration and finance. I literally always expected that I would do something in ministry. Business administration and finance is not where I saw myself — but I know for a fact, a literal fact, that God wants me there." Eli went on to tell them about his dream, about his experience standing face-to-face with Jesus, and they all sat, with their mouths hanging open, taking in his story in amazement. Valerie's eyes filled with tears as she listened to her son's description of Heaven, and the realization that he had, in fact, walked with Jesus during his coma. As he continued talking, Antonne made up his mind that he was going to go for it. If there was ever a place, or a time, when he would be supported and loved, whether he was making the right choice or the wrong choice, this was it.

Julia jokingly added that she wished she would have a supernatural vision or a dream about what she was supposed to do when she grew up. Valerie stood to clear the table while the three young people talked about what it could all mean and what the future might hold for each of them. As Valerie placed the extra biscuits into a plastic storage container, she silently gave God thanks for speaking to her children. She thought about Beau, and quietly asked God to touch his heart and soften his spirit and to make His presence known in Beau's life.

~

For the first time, Beau entered chapel at the rehab facility and sat down quietly in the back row. Every morning, one of the group leaders conducted a small, voluntary Bible study in the facility chapel. This wasn't a regular group meeting. There was no mandatory attendance, there was no evaluation or medical discussion, there was no group sharing — this was a time to "seek truth," that is, if you wanted to seek truth. Beau had never attended one of these Bible studies, and it felt different than being in the chapel during a regular chapel service on Sundays. He expected everyone to turn and stare at him, to possibly mock him or somehow draw attention to the fact that he didn't belong, but no one did. In fact, he actually felt welcomed.

As he listened to the counselor read some Scripture and begin breaking down the passage verse by verse, he found himself willing to talk to God. For the first time in as long as he could remember, he felt compelled to pray. "I don't know what I'm doing here. I don't know if you're even real. I don't know why I'm alive when I should be dead and I don't know why some guys died and I didn't. But, if you're there, I want you to see me. Can you see me? If you're real, I want to know you."

Beau hung his head. He shifted slightly and chastised himself for what he believed to be an inadequate prayer. He felt stupid. He started to stand up and leave, but just as he did, the door to the chapel opened and another man, an Army veteran who he recognized from group sessions, walked in and, despite plenty of empty seats, sat right next to Beau.

After the man made himself comfortable in his seat, out of nowhere, he shifted his weight toward Beau and whispered, "God sees you. God sees us all." It was the first time Beau had heard the man speak at all, and as soon as the words were out of his mouth, he shifted his weight back to the center of his chair and immediately focused on the speaker once again. Beau felt chills form all over his body, but at the same time he felt a warmth and a strange sensation of awe. He wasn't sure what it meant, and he didn't know if he was really ready to believe, but for the first time in years, he felt at peace.

CHAPTER EIGHTEEN

The doorbell rang about five minutes after eight. Julia had just put Gabe to bed and, for the first time in a while, she would have complete control over the remote. She planned to curl up on the sofa and watch something completely girly and as cheesy as possible. Eli and Antonne had gone to the gym and Joe and Valerie had decided on a much needed date night. The whole family was looking forward to family day with Beau, but the event was still too far down the road to prevent her feelings of loneliness. Julia was thankful that she had the McKnight's, thankful that she had met Jesus when she had, and so very grateful for Gabe. She did her best to focus on the blessings in her life, even though the uncertainty of her future threatened her peace of mind regularly. For a split second, she thought about not answering the door. But, her sweet nature would not let her leave someone standing there unattended. She trotted to the large front door, turned the deadbolt and pulled the door open slightly. She scotched the bottom of the door with her foot and peeked out. Ever since she was little girl, she'd been taught to use caution when opening the door. But, as soon as her eyes focused on the visitor, she threw the door open and squealed. She wrapped both her arms around his neck and jumped into him. "Andy!" she squealed with delight. "How? When? We didn't know you were coming!"

Andy laughed. It had been too many months, and he was probably just as excited as Julia was. "To be honest, neither did I."

"Come in! Do you have bags? I'll help you bring in your bags!"

"We can get those later." Andy followed Julia into the house. "Right now, my only priority is the bathroom."

Julia laughed. "Okay, I was just getting ready to watch a chick flick." She laughed again. Her excitement was obvious to Andy, and it warmed his heart.

"I'm always down for a chick flick," Andy said with a shrug and then made a beeline for the restroom.

After just a couple of minutes, Andy returned to the great room and plopped down in the loveseat. Julia sat on the sofa with her feet curled underneath her. She pulled the blanket over her lap and reached for the remote. "At first I was going to text everyone," Julia said, "but then I decided I'm just going to let them be surprised like I was! Is that okay?"

"Fine by me!" Andy responded.

"Okay, so, before we do any movie watching — I want to know what's going on! You're here! I mean, Eli told us you had decided not to reenlist, but last we heard, you didn't really have a plan." Julia put down her phone and leaned in, giving all her attention to Andy.

"That's right," Andy chuckled. "I've been letting God tell me the plan one step at a time. When my time was up, I went and spent a little time back in my hometown. Two days ago, God told me that this was home now and, well, I packed my bags. Mama didn't even get upset. She said she knew it was God. And, since both my parents are retired, I figure they'll be here all the time anyway." He laughed again. "I was hoping Mr. Joe and Ms. Val might put me up until I can find my own place."

"I guarantee they will!" Julia clapped her hands and put both fists in the air like a cheerleader. "I'm so excited!" She lowered her hands and then looked at Andy again, "But, um, did God tell you what you're supposed to *do* here?"

Andy chuckled, "Good question! All I know is that there is some kind of ministry here for me. That's really all I know.

Somewhere around here, God has a job that's got my name on it. I don't know what it is or where it is, but I'll find it." Andy cleared his throat, "Not to change the subject, but what's the latest from Hangdoggy?"

Andy had kept up with Beau as best he could during his final deployment to Afghanistan. He already knew most of what the family had been dealing with, and he knew that Beau had agreed to go to rehab long term. Julia proceeded to tell him about family counseling, about what they learned about trauma and post-traumatic stress disorder and all the other things that could have contributed to Beau's desire to use. They talked extensively about the fact that the rehab they chose was a faith-based organization and their hope was that maybe, just maybe, God might be able to reach Beau there. She told Andy there had been very little contact with Beau so far, but that the updates they had received from the facility were all positive. She told him about family day, and the fact that they have to wait until that day before more regular visits begin. She also told him that eventually, they would all be doing counseling together — with Beau.

Julia filled him in on Antonne's revelation about a career in computer programming and systems, and she tried to tell him about Eli's dream. "There's no way I can do it justice. I'm sure he'll tell you all about it. It is amazing." Andy took it all in, feeling relieved to be there. He had always moved quickly when he knew that he heard God's voice — acting on God's instruction with very little hesitation kept him in the right place at the right time almost every time. He believed this would be no exception. It didn't matter what God would have him do while he was there, he knew he would be fulfilling his purpose in God's call on his life. Julia marveled at Andy's obedience and his willingness to lay it all on the line at the sound of God's voice. But, she also had to admit that she'd never met anyone quite like Andy. She'd never seen anyone who could call out to God and really see things change. He had something special, something that she wanted — a faith that she hoped was contagious.

The pair sat talking for another hour before even bothering to turn on the movie. As the movie played, Andy began to get tired. It had been a long drive, but he wasn't about to drift off. He wanted to be awake when everyone got home. He wanted to see their faces when they walked through the door. Most of all, he wanted to bask in the feeling of being in the center of God's will. He knew he was where he was supposed to be, and this time, the sense of comfort and well-being that accompanied that knowledge was unlike anything he'd ever experienced.

CHAPTER NINETEEN

As Beau walked down the hallway toward the dining room, he couldn't stop thinking about the words of the man from the chapel, "God sees you." Beau hadn't told anyone he felt invisible, and he'd been praying silently that day — hadn't he? How would a total stranger know to use those words at that time? Most of the time he could chalk anything *supernatural* up to coincidence, but that experience had been too much to rationalize away, no matter how hard he tried. He hadn't been able to shake it. In fact, one night, he had lain awake thinking about the man's words, and he wondered if there was anything in the Bible that might explain it. For the first time, he had pulled the Gideon Bible from the drawer in his nightstand and flipped through pages he'd never read. Yes, he knew all the major stories — he was a Sunday School kid, after all — but he'd never studied Scripture on his own. As he skimmed pages, he became frustrated. Where should he start? Some of it felt like a completely different language. What does *begat* even mean? He tossed the Bible back into the drawer and slammed it shut. "I can't even read the Bible right," he thought, dejected. "I'm probably the only grown idiot in the free world who would be better off with a kid's Bible comic book." Feeling inadequate, he had finally drifted off to sleep, and to sooth himself, he decided that the Bible was fine for other people, but it just wasn't for him.

As he turned the corner to the dining room, four different people said 'Hello' and Beau had no choice but to respond. The more time he spent with the counselors and staff at the rehab facility, the more difficult it became for him to run from God. God was everywhere in this place — or at least it seemed that way to Beau. No matter how hard he tried to ignore it or think of other things, he was somehow constantly reminded of faith.

That night, during dinner, the group held a small celebration for a fellow patient who would soon be graduating and who had chosen to move on to the next step of recovery at a local sober-living home. Dale Starnes had been kind to Beau since their very first meeting — he had been kind in the hallway shortly after Beau had begun to experience withdrawal symptoms, when his head was killing him and he felt as though he might throw up, and he had chosen to cuss Dale for saying good morning. He had even been kind when Beau avoided him and blew him off completely during the rest of his first week there. From what Beau could tell, Dale was kind to everyone.

He walked with a marked limp and his right leg was so badly scarred that it reminded Beau of the old olive tree in his grandfather's back yard. During group, Dale had openly shared about his opioid addiction and often spoke about the IED that had nearly taken his leg off during his final deployment, at the end of the final enlistment of his long military career. From his looks, Dale was the last person Beau would have pegged as an addict. He was in his early forties. He had rosy cheeks and a face that could be described as sweet. He seemed smart. He looked like somebody's dad — not a rehab patient. More than once, Dale had spoken about how his addiction started with a choice but became like a parasite that grew inside his veins. He even said that he'd once been the guy who thought all addicts were losers and nothing but trouble — but then he became one.

Dale had committed twenty years of his life to service as a Civil Engineer in the Air Force. He was nearing retirement when he was tasked with one last deployment, backfilling for the Army to facilitate the construction of some new buildings at Bagram Air Base in Kabul. During a routine supply convoy, his vehicle had taken the brunt of the blast from an improvised explosive device. Dale had nearly lost his leg in the attack and admitted that, sometimes, he still wishes he *had*, because if he had lost his leg, he might have avoided the addiction that cost him his marriage and mangled his relationship with his kids. Everyone there knew that Dale had spent the better part of three months focused on reuniting his family. And now that he was graduating and moving on, he and his wife were talking again. Dale's excitement had been obvious when he mentioned that soon he'd be able to take her on a first date all over again.

Beau walked over to the table where everyone was gathered around Dale. They all shared a meal and laughed together. The atmosphere felt hopeful and even Beau couldn't stay silent. He couldn't believe his own ears when he told Dale, "I'm gonna miss you around here," and meant it.

"I'm going to miss you, too!" Dale said. "But not that much." He laughed at his own words and gave Beau a wink. "Hey, walk back to my room with me for a minute, okay?"

Beau was taken aback. He murmured, "Um, okay."

Dale could sense the hesitation in Beau's voice. "Relax kid, it's not the principal's office." He smiled at Beau and turned to the group to say he'd be right back. He headed for the door and Beau followed after him silently. Dale's room was just a short walk from the dining facility and, on the way, Dale asked small-talk type questions to combat the awkwardness of his request. When they arrived at Dale's room, Dale unlocked the door and stepped inside. Beau followed, but waited just about a foot inside the threshold. Dale walked across the room to a small table under the window. Beau took note of the fact that most of Dale's things were already packed up and the room seemed bare and quiet. Dale reached into a small bag that rested on the table. "This was mixed in with some of my stuff. I don't even know where it came from. I definitely don't remember buying it, but I really want you to have it. Don't ask me why I want you to have it, I just do. As soon as I saw it, I felt like it already belonged to you. Weird, huh?"

"Super weird." Beau answered as he reached out his hand. Dale pulled the item from the bag and placed it in Beau's palm. The color drained from Beau's face as he stood staring down at the gift in his hands. It was a book. On the front, Beau saw colorful illustrations surrounding the words "The Action Bible." In the bottom right-hand corner, the words "God's redemptive story" were written in all capital letters. It was a comic book — a Bible comic book. Beau couldn't breathe. How was this even possible? He had been alone in his room, venting his frustrations, when he thought to himself that he would be better off with a Bible comic book more than with an actual Bible — and now *this*?

Dale could see that something about this gift spoke to Beau in a way that he didn't see coming. As a believer, Dale knew that God often worked through people. But, as Dale had told them all multiple times, he was the farthest thing from a *good* Christian that anybody would find. Though he was a believer, Dale hadn't spent nearly enough time pursuing his relationship with God. He credited God with saving his life and helping him get through rehab, but beyond that, he had said very little about his faith. Still, he knew enough to know when to keep his mouth shut. He left Beau standing alone in the middle of his room and quietly made his way to the door. He whispered, "Take all the time you need," just before pulling the door closed behind him.

As he stood there holding that Bible comic book in his hands, Beau felt his knees give way beneath him. As he fell to the floor, he could smell a sweet fragrance in the air and an overwhelming presence began to fill the room. Beau could feel a comforting warmth surrounding him, holding him tightly, as if he were being embraced. The overwhelming sensation of love seemed to pass completely through his body. It was unlike anything Beau had ever experienced, and before he could stop himself, tears were cascading down his cheeks. He hugged the book tightly to his chest and rolled his body forward until his forehead touched the floor in front of him. The tears flowed freely now, as if the dam that had been holding back years of grief and anger had finally broken. Beau could sense a bright light flooding the room around him. The sensation of pure joy began to build in his spirit. He choked back sobs as he attempted to speak, "I'm sorry, I'm so sorry," he cried. "God, please forgive me. I believe. I believe." He managed to get through just a single sentence before he was weeping again. He cried until he was too exhausted to stand. And then, there, face first on the floor, in a pool of his own tears, Beau McKnight stopped running and gave his life to Christ.

CHAPTER TWENTY

"Well, I think it's lovely. Lots of natural light, granite countertops in the bathroom, and it's a really good size." Valerie took the diaper bag from Julia while she unhooked Gabe from his car seat.

"But it's fifteen minutes from here!" Eli spoke up and turned to Andy. "Why don't you just live here? Do you really want to be fifteen minutes away from all this amazingness?" He gestured at his own body and gave a little spin. Antonne broke into laughter. Julia and Valerie joined him.

Andy shook his head and answered, "Fifteen minutes is not that bad. The rent is really good there. And, I mean, I am technically a grown-up, but I have never lived by myself and I kind of want to."

"Okay, but it's your loss." Eli shrugged and slapped Andy on the shoulder as he turned to head inside.

"How are you going to get them to give you that apartment? You ain't even got a job yet." Antonne's question was matter-of-fact — and something that Andy had thought about multiple times.

"Well, I have a deposit and enough for two months of rent. And, God will tell me what to do next." Andy put his hands into his pockets as Valerie made her way down the driveway toward the mailbox.

Antonne reached out and took baby Gabe from Julia. "He gettin' too big for you to carry around all the time." He turned back to Andy and said, "Man, I wish I had that kind of trust. If there's one thing in the world that makes me stressed out, it's money. I've been poor my whole life and I spend most of my time trying to not be poor."

"That's exactly the *opposite* of what God says to do," Andy said.

"Are you coming?" Julia called down the driveway to where Valerie had stopped to open a letter. She had one hand over her mouth and her body language alone told the group that something was definitely up. "Are you okay?"

"Mom?" Eli called out to her as well.

Valerie let the diaper bag fall from her shoulder. It hit the ground with a thud as she felt tears filling her eyes. She started to open her mouth to call out to the others, but all she could get out was a sob. She frantically motioned with her hand and Julia, Antonne, Eli and Andy quickly ran down the driveway to meet her.

"What's wrong?" Eli asked urgently. Valerie handed him the letter, still unable to speak. Eli began reading silently to himself, but when sudden tears caused his eyes to blur, he shoved the letter at Andy, knowing that Andy always seemed to be in control of his emotions. "Read it out loud," he choked out the words.

Dear Mom and Dad – and Julia, Gabe, Eli, and Antonne,

I'll pause and let you get over the initial shock of getting an actual letter from me. I still hate writing stuff by hand, by the way. But this is important.

I want to start just by saying I'm sorry. I'm sorry for everything. I'm sorry for taking my family for granted when I was a kid. Sorry for making choices that wrecked our lives. I'm sorry for not listening to you. Mostly, I'm sorry for wasting so much time on bitterness and anger. I hope that you will all forgive me. I also want you to know that I have finally forgiven myself. I have forgiven myself because I know that God has forgiven me. (Mom, you might want to sit down for this.) Yesterday, I met Jesus. I had an experience unlike anything I expected and unlike anything I have ever had before. (Yes, I'm completely clean and sober, ha ha.) I fell on my face and asked God to forgive me for my sins, and I asked Jesus to be the Lord of my life. I cried. I cried a lot. But I stood up from there a new person. I feel remade. I AM SAVED!

The time I've spent here has been very hard, but also VERY good. I can feel good things coming in my life. I miss you all very much, and I can't wait for family day. I wanted to let you all know first, and I plan to write a letter to Andy later this afternoon. I know I have a lot to learn and a lot of time to make up for. But, that's okay, because I want to.

Julia, I love you. I LOVE you. I am so sorry that I hurt you. I will spend the rest of my life making it up to you. Please kiss Gabe for me and tell him I will see him soon.

Eli, I don't know what to say. You've been my best friend since even before we were born. I'm sorry. Brother, I am so, so sorry. I'm sorry I took you for granted all those times growing up. You always had my back and I took advantage of it. That will never happen again, I promise. I'm sorry for the coma. I'm sorry my stupid choices cost you so much time and stole away the life you should have had. I'm sorry I cost you your future with Ivy. I hope you know I would never hurt you on purpose, but I was an idiot and you paid the price, not just once, but over and over. And somehow you never stopped putting me first. Thank you for being such a great brother. Thank you for always looking out for me. Maybe now I will be strong enough to look out for you sometimes too.

Antonne, you still talk too much – but I love you anyway. I'm sorry I gave you such a hard time. You really are my brother and I wouldn't have it any other way.

Mom and Dad, what can I say? There are no words to say thank you enough times for making sure that I always have what I need, for taking care of me, for raising me in a Godly household. Here, in this place, it's clear to me what a good life I have had so far and I am so sorry for taking it for granted. I will never do that again.

I can't wait to see you all at family day! We will have telephone access after that and I will be able to call you. If you talk to Mimi or Nana, please tell them my good news. They will tell everyone we know and I won't have to write any more letters, haha!

See you soon,
Love, Beau

As Andy reached the end of the letter, he lifted both arms into the air, still grasping the paper in his right hand. He let his head fall back as he looked up toward the sky and silently praised God for what they'd just learned. Antonne sniffed back tears and let out a yell so loud that even the neighbors could hear. He began dancing around in the driveway as the rest of the family laughed and cried at the same time. Julia jumped up and down as she hugged Val. Valerie's tears had flowed so heavily that they'd caused her mascara to run, staining her cheeks in two long, black streaks. Eli pressed his palms to his eyes, wiping back tears. He began to laugh as he stepped toward his mom and Julia and wrapped his big arms around them both. Valerie realized, in that moment, that his arms were no longer frail or thin. He was the picture of health. She silently gave thanks to God for seeing her through it all and bringing her to this moment. "Joe! I have to call Joe!" she shouted. "Oh, what am I saying? I'll just drive to the office!" She beamed. "Tonight, we celebrate! Who wants to go out for dinner?"

"What kind of a question is *that*?" Eli answered. "When have we ever said 'no'?" he laughed, wiping his cheeks with his hands to brush away the tears that had puddled there. "I just realized something." Eli looked at Andy and chuckled, "Beau wrote you a letter and you're already here. He literally hates writing stuff by hand. I don't know why, but I find that kinda funny."

"Don't anybody tell him," Andy laughingly said in return.

Valerie handed the rest of the mail to Eli and turned to get back in the car. She couldn't wait to see Joe's face when he read the news. "You all decide on a dinner spot. Julia, maybe we can go to the mall after and look for something to wear to Kevin's wedding!"

Julia was still speechless. Her heart was swelling inside her chest to the point of bursting. Everything she'd wanted, and everything she'd prayed for, since the day Beau McKnight walked back into her life seemed to become a reality in that one, single moment. Suddenly, her life felt surreal. She just nodded at Valerie because she still couldn't speak.

Valerie smiled back at her. Peace flooded her spirit. For months, she'd been telling herself that God would take care of them and that everything would be okay. Now, peering through the windshield of her car, staring at the next generation of believers in her driveway, she *knew* He was true to His word.

CHAPTER TWENTY-ONE

Joe was up before the sun on the morning of family day at the center. He was more excited than a kid on Christmas morning. The anticipation of throwing his arms around Beau and celebrating his newfound faith was almost more than he could stand. "I wonder if they'd open up early if I showed up early?" he thought, as he sipped his coffee by the bay window. He loved the look of his own back yard in the early morning. The way the mist rose off the pool and the lights danced off the water while the sun rose slowly from the east made him thankful for his blessings every time he saw it. He decided to pass the time by making a big breakfast for his family. He picked up his phone and texted Andy to invite him to breakfast, <BIG BREAKFAST IN THE MAKING. HOPE TO SEE YOU HERE.> Andy had been settled into his new apartment for about a week. Joe was surprised when he got an immediate return message, <WOULDN'T MISS IT.> Andy had always been an early riser, and the Marines had instilled that quality in him even further. These days, getting up early felt like second nature to Andy, and his grandmother had always told him that early morning was the best time to spend with the Lord. Sometimes Andy chose dedicated Bible study. Sometimes he just sat quietly and waited on God to speak to his spirit.

Andy was probably as excited for family day as Joe was. The McKnights had kept Andy's presence a secret from Beau. He had no idea that Longview had become Andy's home after he left the Marines. Beau and Andy had exchanged a few letters since Beau's stint in rehab began, but none since Andy had moved to Longview. Beau had no idea Andy and Eli had been hanging out together nearly every afternoon, and he certainly didn't anticipate Andy showing up at family day. Andy was nearly beside himself anticipating Beau's reaction, though you'd never know it based on his chronically calm demeanor.

Joe pulled Valerie's large skillet from under the cabinet and placed it on top of the stove. He went to the fridge and began gathering his supplies, hoping that he could manage to start breakfast without waking the rest of his family. A few minutes later, Antonne came sleepily up the stairs. "Oh no, did I wake you?"

"No sir. I just woke up and couldn't go back to sleep," Antonne responded.

"I know the feeling," Joe chuckled. "There's coffee if you want some." Antonne didn't really drink coffee, instead he drank flavored creamer with a splash of coffee.

"That sounds great!" Antonne walked to the cabinet and pulled down a coffee cup. "Mr. Joe, it's been a while since I said thank you. But, thank you, for all of this. It really is more than I could've hoped for."

"I love having you here Antonne. I wouldn't have it any other way." Joe began beating eggs in a bowl. It had been a really long time since he'd cooked, and since he didn't want to burn anything, he decided that scrambled eggs would be the safest option.

Over the course of the next twenty minutes, Julia came down the stairs with Gabe on her hip, Eli bounded into the room like a little boy, and Valerie strolled in with a smile on her face that told everyone *nothing* could ruin her good mood. Andy arrived dressed in jeans, boots and a polo shirt. He wore a baseball cap pulled low across his forehead, but he kept his hair short enough that if he needed to remove it, there would be no surprises. Over breakfast, the girls discussed what they would wear for the day, tried to determine whether or not they should take Gabe's large stroller or the umbrella stroller, and everyone speculated over what the day's events might hold. For the most part, the events didn't matter — all that mattered was being with Beau.

~

The McKnight clan passed under a giant banner that said "Welcome Family." They crossed through two large double doors as they entered the atrium outside the auditorium. They were told they had two options for an opening lecture. One lecture was specifically for families that had been attending counseling through the facility. The other lecture was for families that had not participated in the counseling program. Families were informed that, after their respective lectures, they would meet up with their loved ones in the courtyard behind the building. From there, they had several options as to how they would progress through the afternoon. Joe and Valerie led the way into the lecture hall for families that had been attending counseling and the rest of their group followed behind them. Julia made it a point to sit near the end, just in case Gabe became fussy.

As the lecture began, Julia found herself distracted. She did her best to stay focused, but all she could think about was seeing Beau again. The speaker for the event was a pastor who also served as a sort of chaplain for patients at the facility. He was well spoken, funny, and the tone of his voice commanded the room. The lecture was informative and interesting. Andy seemed to be extremely invested in the speaker's comments. Eli could see his wheels turning and wondered what was going through his mind as he listened.

After the lecture was over, Valerie and Julia excused themselves to the restroom. Julia used the time to change Gabe's diaper and make a bottle. She looked at herself in the mirror for what felt like a long time. She fluffed her hair and pulled a compact from her purse so she could powder her nose. Valerie applied some lipstick and then checked her eye makeup in the mirror. When they walked back into the atrium, they found all the guys waiting for them. They instinctively followed the crowd of people heading down the sidewalk toward the rear of the building. As they turned the corner, they could see the courtyard where round tables covered with white tablecloths and white folding chairs were placed to accommodate all the families. There was music playing, and each of the tables had centerpieces consisting of three helium balloons in various colors. There were several food trucks lined up along the perimeter of the courtyard, and the smell of good food floated on the light breeze. As they grew closer to the tables, Valerie could see place cards marked with the last names of various families on each of the round tables. "It looks like we have assigned tables." Antonne walked ahead of her and began scanning the place cards for the McKnight name. Andy decided to follow suit and began checking tables around the perimeter.

"I found it!" Antonne called out. The group made their way toward the table and Julia decided to open the umbrella stroller for Gabe. She wondered if he would fall asleep before he got to see his daddy. "This is great!" Antonne added. "I saw a barbecue truck over there." Eli laughed and he jokingly picked up one of the place settings from the table and held a knife in one hand and a fork in the other as if he was saying, "Let's eat!" Andy was smiling as he pulled out his chair and started to sit down. But, before he could put his rear end in the seat, he saw Beau — his stature and stride unmistakable — making his way down the sidewalk toward them.

"I see him!" Andy didn't bother to sit down, instead he stood tall watching Beau as he approached. It was obvious that Beau had a new countenance. He was practically glowing. His head was up, his shoulders were back and he had a smile on his face. As long as Andy had known Beau, he had never seen him smile like that. Joe, Valerie, Julia and Eli all stood. Valerie couldn't help herself, she began to wave and tears welled in her eyes when she saw Beau wave back.

Beau picked up his pace. He began to jog toward his family and Valerie began moving toward him. He wrapped his arms around her and lifted her off the ground, "Mom! I missed you!"

"I missed you more!" Valerie kissed his cheek three times in short succession. Joe stepped in behind Val and held his arms open wide. Beau stepped into them without hesitation. The father and son stood, holding each other, for a long time — longer than they had since Beau was a little boy. When Beau finally stepped back, he had tears in his eyes. Naturally, Joe did too. And then, Beau saw Andy.

"Hangdoggy!" Andy shouted as he raised his arms to greet Beau. Beau's mouth fell open as he moved toward Andy. The shock of Andy's presence was written all over Beau's face, but his shock was nothing compared to his joy and excitement at seeing his best friend. It was obvious that keeping Andy's family day attendance a secret had made Beau's day, and the entire family could feel the love between them as they greeted each other.

"What? What are you doing here?" Beau asked as he wrapped both his arms around his friend and smiled from ear to ear.

"Where else would I be?" Andy asked. Beau reached out and roughed the top of Andy's head. Then Eli stepped forward.

He couldn't wait another minute, and he couldn't stop smiling, none of them could. Eli didn't even wait for Beau to hug him — he didn't even wait for Beau to open his arms — he grabbed his brother around the shoulders with every ounce of strength he had. He squeezed him and buried his forehead into Beau's shoulder. Everyone in the group could see the change in Beau. He seemed lighter and happier and at peace.

Julia and Valerie were both sniffling by the time Beau made his way around the table to Julia. Julia leaned down and lifted Gabe out of the stroller. Beau reached for him instantly. He held Gabe close to his chest, pressing his lips to the top of his son's head. He inhaled deeply through his nose, as if he was breathing Gabe into himself. Julia could see the tears filling his eyes as he held his son, quietly swaying back and forth in a moment that was so beautiful it couldn't possibly be put into words. Then, he shifted Gabe to one side and turned toward Julia. He wrapped his arm around her waist and pulled her close to him. He bent down toward her, but instead of kissing her immediately, he placed his forehead against hers and whispered, "You are stunning." He kissed her tenderly on the lips, and she wiped a tear from her cheek before she wrapped her arms around him and just held on to him while he held Gabe.

As the afternoon wore on, the family shared food, laughter, and love. They filled Beau in on everything happening at home, about the upcoming wedding and all about Andy's moving into his apartment. They laughed until they were crying as Antonne told the story of Andy and Eli and their attempt to carry Andy's bed up the stairs and how Andy was trapped in the corner when the box springs became wedged between the ceiling and the wall on the way up. Later, Beau shared the story of his salvation, about his secret prayers, the man in the chapel and the comic book Bible, and left them all speechless — even Andy — who had listened with a smile on his face so big he was almost unrecognizable.

Beau went on to tell them that since that first night, he spent as much time as he could learning what it really meant to follow Jesus. He shared with them that he, somehow, no longer felt worthless, that he knew everything was going to be okay, and that he had a purpose. "In fact, I have a job to do," he said. "A job that is bigger than any career I can think of. And, I don't know how I'll feel once I leave here, it may get harder, but right now I really can't even imagine taking even a single pill or taking a drink. It's like that desire was never there in the first place — like it's just *gone*. I feel like a brand new person."

Joe had always been proud of his sons. But in that moment, he was probably more proud of Beau than he had ever been. Beau was articulate, full of life and radiating with what could only be described as joy. Valerie was either laughing or crying pretty much the entire time.

"So? What is it? What job?" Eli asked eagerly.

"I'm glad you asked, because I was thinking about it, but didn't want to be the one to bring it up," Antonne said impatiently. Beau laughed lightly.

Julia leaned her head onto Beau's shoulder as he began to speak "Well, the truth is, I am kind of scared to say it out loud because it sounds crazy. And I literally have no business even considering it."

Andy spoke up, "God always gives people stuff that's more than they can do on their own — that's how you know it's God."

"Really?" Beau asked.

"Yeah, of course," Andy responded. "Abraham made a baby when he was ancient, Paul went from beating Christians to leading them, Rahab was a hooker for crying out loud!" Everyone laughed at Andy's emphasis on the word 'hooker.' "I mean, Hangdoggy, you're a lot of things, but you ain't a hooker." Beau couldn't help but laugh. He nodded his head and looked down at Gabe who was sitting on his lap and still eating small chunks of French fries from the table. He pressed his lips to the top of Gabe's head and took a deep breath.

"Just tell us already!" Eli added. The anticipation was getting to him. Eli was practically floating. He had his brother back and the relief in his heart took one hundred pounds off his psyche.

"Okay. Well," Beau hesitated, rubbing his right shoulder, which had become a habit after his most recent surgery. "I think I'm supposed to start a veteran's service. A mission, like a faith-based organization to help them with rehab, therapy, finding jobs, making resumes, counseling, even recreation and getting them off the streets." He took a deep breath. "The VA can only do so much. I've heard so much about the gaps in the system since I've been here. There's such a need, and after hearing all the stories, I really feel like I could help meet that need — but I literally have no idea where to start. I am a veteran, but that's really the extent of my qualifications," he laughed. "Like, oh yeah, let *me* help you get your whole life together because I'm *so* qualified." The group laughed, but Joe was the first to speak.

"I think it's an admirable calling, son. A big one, but a good one."

"Thanks, Dad," Beau said with a slight smile.

Eli had been silent for a long time before he finally spoke. When he finally opened his mouth, his eyes lit up,

"You'll probably need someone to help you with administration and finances, right?"

"Eli! That's a great idea!" Valerie added with excitement.

"Seriously, what if this is what my dream was all about?" he added excitedly.

"Wait, what?" Beau asked.

Eli went on to tell Beau about his dream, about waking up with a calling on his life but no idea where that calling would fit and, as he spoke, they all marveled at how well the two visions fit together.

After a few more minutes, Antonne spoke up, "What about a computer guy? You might need that, too, right?"

"Yes!" Beau shouted. He was becoming more excited as the conversation wore on. "But, do you know one? It can't just be any ol' hack you know," he said sarcastically as he ribbed Antonne.

"Well, not yet, you big jerk!" Antonne answered with a laugh as he punched Beau's arm.

"What about me?" Julia added. "I want in on this action." She bubbled over with excitement and anticipation at the idea of being part of something bigger than herself. "I am really good on the phone! I could be an office manager, maybe."

"You could be whatever you want to be!" Beau said. "You're smarter than you give yourself credit for." He kissed her cheek.

"You can't go wrong when you listen to God," Andy added. "Which is why I think I should throw my hat into this ring too." Everyone looked in Andy's direction. Valerie was beaming, so much had happened over the course of a single hour. She felt her heart swelling with pride. Joe leaned back in his chair and crossed his arms. He felt as if his boys were making up for years of lost time right before his eyes. The practical side of him wanted to chime in and keep them all *grounded*, to talk with them about the business side of things, about funding and taxes and all the red tape, but his spirit prompted him to keep his mouth shut. There would be plenty of time for that talk later.

Andy continued, "I know I'm called to ministry and right now it's like my soul is screaming at me, 'This is it!' So I guess I'm applying for the job."

"You're hired!" Beau jumped up. "I don't know what that means yet, but the job is yours!"

"I think we can really do this, guys," Julia added. "I mean really."

"We have a long way to go, but I really think we're onto something here," Eli added. "There's going to be a lot to consider and a lot of, you know, adulting type stuff to do, but I think we can do it." Joe smiled when he heard Eli's statement, a chip off the 'ol block.

"Everybody starts somewhere!" Beau exclaimed.

A moment later, Beau stood up and pushed in his chair. "What's happening?" Valerie asked. "Where are you off to?"

"You mean, 'Where are *we* off to?'" Beau answered. "I have a surprise for you." Julia clapped her hands and stood up. She took Gabe from Beau's arms and put him in the stroller.

"What?" Val asked with excitement.

"There's a baptism in the chapel — and it's mine!" Beau answered.

CHAPTER TWENTY-TWO

When the day of Kevin's wedding finally arrived, Beau had been thriving in his sober-living home for two weeks. He arrived at his parent's house dressed in gray slacks, a white button down shirt and a powder blue tie. He rang the doorbell and Valerie answered, her hair still wrapped in a towel. "Beau! You look fantastic. Why in the world would you ring the doorbell? This is still your house!" She hugged her son tightly and said, "I have to go finish up, it's been crazy here this morning." Beau walked through the door to find Gabe playing in the floor. He looked adorable in his little khakis and suspenders. Eli was sitting on the hearth, bouncing one of Gabe's light up balls off the floor and catching it in his right hand over and over again. Joe was sitting in his chair talking on the phone and Andy was in the kitchen. Beau could see him at the table with his Bible open in front of him.

"Yes, sir," Joe said. "We're very interested, but we have some big hoops to jump through before we even get to that point... Yes. Thank you. That's fantastic news. These guys are going to lose their minds!" Joe laughed before he said his goodbyes and hung up the phone. "Guys!" he yelled. "Everybody get in here, quick!" Andy and Antonne ran into the room from the kitchen as though an emergency siren had gone off.

Eli jumped, startled. He dropped the ball and stood quickly, "What is it? What's wrong?" Valerie rushed out of her room and stood at the top of the stairs. She was dressed in sapphire blue. Her dress was a boat-neck that exposed her collarbones and skimmed her body to the floor. "What in the world is it now?" she asked, as she ran her brush through her hair.

Julia walked down the open hall toward her, dressed in a simple red gown fitted to the knee. She carried a pair of heels in her fingers and added, "What in the world?"

Andy, Joe, Beau, Eli and Antonne were congregated in the great room, their attention drawn to the top of the stairs. Every man in the room was dumbstruck at the sight of the women. "Wow!" Beau said.

"I second that," Joe added. "We are some blessed men," he said, as he slapped Beau on the back.

"Aww," Julia said.

"You're looking pretty good yourself there handsome," Val added, "but you didn't about give me a heart attack just to tell us how good we look." She fluffed her hair with her hand one last time and set her brush on the table at the top of the stairs.

"Oh right!" Joe said as he remembered why he had yelled for them. "That was Henry Samford on the phone, Henry Samford, boys — you know, of Samford Real Estate?" Only Valerie reacted with a gasp. The young people didn't seem as impressed. "Pastor Brian told him about our vision for the veteran's ministry and told him our story. He said he'd been praying about it for about a week and he wants to donate one of his office buildings to us! He said he has several in mind and wants us to pick the one we want!"

"What?" Beau shouted. "That's incredible!"

"Are you serious?" Eli added. "You can't be serious? I mean, what? Do you know what that would mean for us?" He looked back and forth between Beau and his father. Both brothers were beaming.

"I told him we weren't anywhere near that point yet, but he said he wants to be part of what we're building. He's a Navy vet himself, you know. Anyway, he said this is his way of supporting the ministry! At first, I told him that was too much, but he said we'd actually be doing him a favor on property taxes," Joe laughed. Andy hugged Antonne on the spot and shouted out loud with joy. Beau was so shocked at this, Andy was always so calm. To hear Andy shout with excitement made him laugh.

"God is just so, so good! Right? I mean, right?" Andy asked. "How could you not be excited?" He looked around the room. Julia and Val made their way down the stairs and the family shared a moment of surprised celebration.

Beau marveled at the fact that, in a matter of weeks, what had started as a vision for his future had become an active part of his life — and his whole family was involved. Before long, he would be back home with his family, taking some classes and actively working on a new veterans' service ministry. He shook his head and laughed to himself, "Ministry," he thought. "Never in a million years would I have imagined myself going into ministry." He smiled and reached out to pull Gabe up into his arms. His shoulder made it difficult, he still had pain and his range of motion was still limited, but what he lacked in physical ability, he made up for in sheer will. Thus far, his desire to self-medicate had all but disappeared. And though he expected to face temptation, he believed that, with God's help, he would be strong enough to withstand it.

"Are we ready to go?" Joe asked, as Val grabbed her evening bag from the coffee table.

"We are!" Valerie watched as all of her *kids* made their way out the front door. She silently gave thanks to God for how far they'd come and she thanked him in advance for the promise of a beautiful future.

~

The wedding was a massive affair. Eli had no idea how many lives the Hinkley family had impacted over the years, but it seemed as though everyone in town had been invited. Maggie was absolutely beautiful in her gown and Kevin seemed unexpectedly dapper in his mess dress uniform. The reception hall was decorated beautifully, no expense had been spared on the floral centerpieces and up lighting on every column. Beau had been the center of attention since the reception began, and his captivating personality had returned in full force. He was the life of the party once again, only this time he was completely sober. Eli watched him interacting with Julia, he watched his parents doting over his nephew and he watched Antonne hitting on every woman he met — never mind the fact that he didn't know anyone outside of the McKnight family. Andy seemed to feel a little out of place. But one of Maggie's bridesmaids had taken a shine to him and Eli could tell Andy didn't mind in the least.

Just before dinner was served, the doors to the hall opened, and a beautiful brunette dressed in emerald green stepped inside. Eli hadn't expected to see Ivy. He didn't even know she was back in town. His breath caught in his chest as he watched her move across the room. He glanced back at the door, waiting for Mark to walk through behind her — but he didn't.

Ivy walked across the room and greeted Maggie and Kevin. Eli couldn't hear her, but he could imagine her voice as she apologized for missing the ceremony and gave them each a hug. She walked to the gift table and pulled a card from her evening bag. Then she began to scan the room. Eli pulled his eyes away, he didn't want her to catch him staring. Within moments, she was on the move again. She had spotted Joe and Valerie across the room. Eli watched the exchange between his parents and Ivy. Then, he saw his mother pointing in his direction. He panicked and turned his face away quickly, looking for somewhere — anywhere to go. It was too late, Ivy had spotted him. He began to feel his heart beating rapidly as she walked toward him across the dance floor.

As Ivy walked, her stomach began doing flips. She smoothed her dress with her hand and fidgeted nervously with the small hook on her evening bag. She tried to look calm, but inside, she was falling apart. Eli looked, well, he looked perfect. He looked strong. He was clean shaven and his hair was neat. His skin was smooth and his jawline was chiseled. He looked healthy — nothing like the frail version of himself she'd left sitting alone in the hospital courtyard. What would she say when she reached him? It felt like the longest walk of her life.

Eli's palms grew sweaty immediately. When he saw Ivy's long hair moving with her stride, he was transported back in time and he felt almost sick to his stomach. He wanted to run away. He didn't think he'd be able to handle hearing about her happy new life with Mark. He wanted her to be happy, but he didn't want the details — his heart simply couldn't bear it. Sure, he had been on a few dates since the day Ivy broke his heart. He'd even braved a blind date with the daughter of one of his mother's friends from her book club. But, no matter how hard he tried, nobody ever made him forget about Ivy. In fact, it had taken a literal act of God to replace her. And the only time he had stopped pining for her was while God was using him to protect Julia's life — and when that moment was past, his feelings for Ivy returned, almost as quickly as they'd gone. No one made him both nervous and calm at the same time —

except Ivy. Eli didn't realize he was holding his breath until Ivy spoke to him.

"Hi," Ivy said. Her voice was hesitant.

"Hi," Eli answered. He put his hands into his pockets in the hopes of looking composed.

"You look fantastic," Ivy was sincere when she spoke. "It's so good to see you."

"It's good to see you too. You look great." She did look great, too great. She had grown into a breathtaking woman. To Eli, she had always been breathtaking — but seeing her here, after missing her for so long, made her beauty all the more obvious to him.

"Thank you," she said. "I was actually hoping to see you here."

"Really?" Eli asked. He was trying to look nonchalant, but his discomfort was obvious. Ivy glanced around the room. She noticed several sets of eyes on them, including Beau's. No wonder Eli felt uncomfortable.

"I... Do you think we could maybe go somewhere and talk? Outside maybe? There are, well, there are things to say." Eli could hear the sincerity in her voice.

"Um, okay." He shrugged and gestured toward the door. He could feel half the room watching them as they left. They walked down the sidewalk toward the fountain. Even the outside of the hall was beautiful. Eli took a deep breath. He made a mental note of their romantic surroundings and reminded himself of how it felt the day she walked away. "Well," he said. "We're outside — are you sure Mark won't be upset?" He emphasised Mark's name.

"I highly doubt it," she replied. "He's in Africa with his fiancé, Susan." She scoffed and then shrugged.

"What?" Eli asked. "Fiancé?"

"Yep. They got engaged last month, after dating about a month." She sighed before she continued. "We were never right for each other," she paused, "because he was never you." She hesitated before she continued, allowing Eli room to speak if he wanted to, but Eli had nothing to say. He just stared at her, but she could tell that he wanted her to continue. "I was always comparing him to you. I couldn't help myself." She paused again, "Look, Eli, when I first went to Africa I was just caught up. I was lonely. I was worried. Everyone told me you may never wake up. And then Mark was there, and I don't know. I was so confused. But then, after everything that happened between you and me, I went back to Africa with Mark and the novelty wore off because he just wasn't you. It didn't take long for me to realize that I'd made a massive mistake — the biggest of my life. It wasn't fair to him, and I got so tired of faking it.

In the end, he got tired of being compared to you every day too."

She looked away for a moment. "My call into overseas missions seems to have run its course too. I loved my time in Africa, but as soon as I went back the second time, I knew I wasn't supposed to be there. I think it was only meant for me for a little while. After Mark and I ended things, I came back to Texas and enrolled in a few classes. I wanted to call you, but I didn't know what to say. I didn't know how to tell you that I'd hurt you for no reason and that I'd been so, so wrong. I've been hiding from you ever since." She paused again. Eli remained silent. "I've even made myself go out on dates a few times since I got back, but nobody worth mentioning." She took a breath, "I'm sorry, I'm rambling." She turned back to face him, "What about you? Is there a plus one here somewhere?" She smiled and looked back toward the reception hall.

Eli wasn't sure what to say. He'd only been out on a few dates since she shattered his heart and he'd fallen uncontrollably, albeit briefly, in love with his own brother's girlfriend, but he certainly didn't plan to tell Ivy about it. If he had his way, he'd never speak of it again. It saved Julia's life, so he knew it was a God thing, but it still made Eli feel like a terrible brother. He shook his head. "Nothing worth mentioning," he said, keeping it short. He was doing his best to refrain from showing any emotion.

"Eli, I know you have no reason to even listen to me, and you'd be well within your rights to walk away right now — but the truth is, I have missed you. I only really came tonight because I was hoping maybe we could try again." She reached for his hand and slowly rubbed her thumb across his fingers. I have been too afraid to call you and I know I don't deserve it, but do you think maybe you could forgive me and maybe we could start over?

Eli stayed quiet for a few minutes. To Ivy, it felt like hours. This moment had been all he'd wanted for so long, but now that it was happening, he was afraid. He didn't want to risk heartbreak again, it had been too hard. For a split second, he thought about saying no, but as he stood there, looking into her eyes, he knew she was still everything he wanted. He knew his love for her was still part of God's plan for his life. Before he could answer, she nervously spoke again, "I guess it's true what they say, you really *don't* know what you have until it's gone."

"I knew what I had," Eli replied. He interlaced his fingers with hers and squeezed her hand. He knew there would still be things to say. He knew they'd have to rebuild what they once had, but he also knew they'd have a lifetime to do it.

EPILOGUE

Antonne sat at the kitchen table with his laptop open in front of him. He was typing away when Valerie walked into the room to place her coffee mug in the sink.

"I'm sorry, I should be helping," Antonne said. "I just really need to get this done before the party starts. We've been having some trouble with the admissions and accounting systems at the center and since Beau got us that contract with the city, it really needs to be perfect. Eli will never let me live it down if that online payment system goes down again." He laughed and shrugged his shoulders.

In a few short years, Antonne had gone from reluctantly studying computer technology, to absolute guru. He truly had a supernatural talent for computer systems and programming and the Legacy of Valor Veteran's Ministry had been reaping the benefits since day one.

"Don't you worry about it, hon. We've got plenty of time." Valerie walked over and patted his shoulder.

"Look what came in the mail today!" Joe ran into the kitchen. He waved a large, manila envelope in the air and Valerie began to jump up and down. He handed the envelope to Antonne, who knew immediately what it was.

Antonne stood to his feet. His eyes became immediately teary. As he carefully raised the metal tabs on the envelope, he looked up to see Joe putting his arm around Val's waist as they watched. He slid the document from the envelope and read the name aloud, "Antonne Quentin Young McKnight." He turned the paper around and showed Joe and Val. It was an official copy of his new birth certificate. Joe and Val moved in to hug him instantly. When Antonne had first met Beau, he never would have guessed they'd one day be brothers. Then on his birthday, Joe and Valerie had surprised him with adoption papers. It had been one of the best days of Antonne's life and now, at long last, he could prove he was officially a McKnight.

Andy walked through the door of the kitchen behind a collection of powder blue balloons. "Beau and Julia will be here with the kids in a few minutes," he said. "Apparently, Levi took a longer nap than usual and Julia said she just couldn't make herself wake him up. She didn't say so, but I can tell she's tired. I think their anniversary trip next week will do her some good. The ministry is growing so fast, she hasn't been able to take enough time off since Levi was born."

"I'm so glad they're going to be able to get away," Joe said. "Beau loves his work so much, getting him to take a vacation is like pulling teeth!"

Piper walked in behind Andy, trying to maneuver a collection of pink balloons as she walked. In the months since she and Andy had become "official," she'd come to love the McKnights and they loved her. She was quickly becoming one of the family. Andy suspected she might be *the one*, but he had no plans to rush the relationship. Piper placed her set of balloons on one end of the table and began carefully scanning the framed photos that were strategically placed along the buffet line. "Andy! You officiated their wedding?" She picked up a picture of Eli and Ivy during their wedding to take a closer look.

Andy smiled, "I did! I did Beau and Julia's wedding too." He stepped closer to look with her. "Once I was ordained, I became the official McKnight wedding doer." Piper laughed and leaned her head against his shoulder for a brief moment.

Valerie stuck her head in close to Andy and whispered, "Who will we get to do your wedding? You can't marry yourself." She nudged him and winked. He shot her a wide-eyed look and put his finger to his lips to shush her. She giggled and returned to her task of placing desserts on the table.

Gabe came running around the corner and jumped into Joe's arms, "Papa! We just got here and do you know who got here too?"

"Who?" Joe asked, acting as though he was riveted on every word his grandson said.

"Uncle Eli! Uncle Eli is here! And so is Aunt Ivy. He leaned in to Joe and whispered, "Aunt Ivy's belly is very full." Gabe puffed his cheeks out with air and held it. Joe burst into laughter.

"Shh!" Joe said as Julia came into the room behind him with little Levi in her arms. Antonne jumped up and ran to take him from her.

"There's my little homey. I've been waiting for you to get here!" Antonne said as he cradled the baby and kissed his small head. He kissed Julia on the cheek and quickly returned to the table. Beau entered the kitchen behind her and placed the diaper bag on the counter. His smile was infectious.

"Guess what," he said, beaming. "I just found out that Legacy was named Service Organization of the Year! They're sending a news crew out next week and everything! Can you believe it?"

"It's so exciting!" Julia added.

"That's amazing!" Andy chimed in.

Eli and Ivy finally came through the door of the kitchen. Eli walked with his hand on the small of Ivy's back. Her belly was round and perfect under her long, sky-blue dress. Eli wore a light pink shirt with the words "team girl" written across the front. For several months he had joked that only a girl could make Ivy that nauseous. Hugs were exchanged all around and everyone commented on how beautiful Ivy looked. Gabe ran to Uncle Eli and Eli threw him into the air and tickled him, pretending to count his ribs. The group celebrated together and spent just a few minutes discussing work, which didn't feel like work at all.

Eli's tenderness toward his wife was obvious and it made Val proud. "He'll make such a wonderful father," she whispered to Joe, who emphatically agreed. Val had never organized a gender reveal party before, but she couldn't be more excited. The guests would soon be arriving and it wouldn't be long until she learned whether or not her next grandchild would be a boy or a girl.

Don't worry, the McKnights will be back! Stay tuned for new releases by Tylie Vaughan Eaves.

Watch for her next series, coming soon!

AUTHOR'S NOTE

Thus far in my life, I have yet to do anything one hundred percent flawlessly. This book is no exception. I have done my best to present accuracy and continuity in every line, but if you search for mistakes, you'll likely find them.

I should also add that this is a work of fiction. Names, characters, events and incidents are either the products of my imagination or used in a fictitious manner. Any resemblance to actual persons, living or dead, or actual events is purely coincidental.

WHAT I BELIEVE

As this is a work of *Christian* fiction, I would be remiss not to share the greatest news I've ever received – Christ. I believe in the One living God, and Jesus Christ as God in the flesh. I believe Christ died on the cross at the hands of sinful man to redeem me (all of us) from our sin and to restore our perfect relationship with the Father. I believe in *every* promise of Scripture. I believe in miracles – I've lived them. I believe God wants to bless us – I walk in it. I believe He wants us to live lives full of joy. I believe He wants the best for us. And I believe loving others means sharing this news, come what may.

THE PLAN OF SALVATION

Accepting this gift is simple – Once you've chosen to trust Christ as your Savior, and you truly believe in your heart that God loves you, that He sent His son, Jesus, to die as redemption for your sins, and that Christ rose again to conquer the grave, all you have to do is confess that belief.

"9 If you declare with your mouth, "Jesus is Lord," and believe in your heart that God raised him from the dead, you will be saved. 10 For it is with your heart that you believe and are justified, and it is with your mouth that you profess your faith and are saved." Romans 10:9-10

Once you've done these things, it's time to live as a Christ follower. It's challenging, but it's the most amazing, rewarding adventure I've ever been on. Get into the Bible, find like-minded people, and take active steps to resist sin and to grow in your faith. Once you see what God has in store for your life, you, too, will want to shout it from the rooftops – I guarantee it.

Made in the USA
Columbia, SC
17 December 2019

85110217R00126